"Della Stout?"

She nodded. "Yes. I'm Della. And you are?"

He held out his hand. "I'm Clement White. It's a pleasure to meet ya, Miss Stout."

She shook his hand quickly, then pulled away. "These are my bags."

While he tried to figure how he could carry all her luggage at once, she looked him up and down beneath hooded eyes. He certainly was handsome, in a dull, country kind of way. He had nothing on the dashing Robert Wilkins—not that she cared one jot for Robert, after the way he'd treated her.

She followed him dejectedly through the rain along the platform, then down the slippery steps to the muddy street beyond. When she didn't see a cab waiting for them, she shook her head. Was she to slosh through all this mud like a common vagabond? Apparently he expected her to, and she had no choice but to follow him. He was already disappearing across the street, buried beneath a mound of carpetbags and luggage, and didn't turn back to check on her progress. She'd soon lose sight of him if she didn't keep up.

Vivi Holt lives in beautiful Brisbane, Australia, with her husband, three children and their three guinea pigs. After a career as a knowledge manager, she is now living her dream of writing full-time. When she's not writing, she loves to hike, read, sing and travel. As a former student of history, Vivi especially enjoys creating unique and thrilling tales inspired by true historical events.

COWBOYS
AND DEBUTANTES:
AN ANTHOLOGY

VIVI HOLT

FEATURING: Della & Hattie

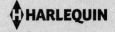

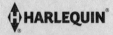

ISBN-13: 978-1-335-93737-7

Cowboys and Debutantes: An Anthology

Copyright © 2020 by Harlequin Books S.A.

Della
First published in 2017 by Vivi Holt. This edition published in 2020.
Copyright © 2017 by Vivi Holt

Hattie
First published in 2017 by Vivi Holt. This edition published in 2020.
Copyright © 2017 by Vivi Holt

Recycling programs for this product may not exist in your area.

This edition published by arrangement with Harlequin Books S.A.

For questions and comments about the quality of this book, please contact us at CustomerService@Harlequin.com.

Harlequin Enterprises ULC
22 Adelaide St. West, 40th Floor
Toronto, Ontario M5H 4E3, Canada
www.Harlequin.com

Printed in U.S.A.

CONTENTS

DELLA

Chapter One

April 1888

Della Eustice Stout knew two things in life. The first was that a girl could become a spinster in less time than it took a hansom cab to get from Grand Central Station to the Brooklyn Bridge. And the second was that if Uncle Ulysses was so upset he had to send her home before he could talk about it with Aunt Fanny, then something was terribly, terribly wrong.

She grabbed hold of her straw hat, the large feather on it tickling the side of her neck as she ran. The other hand clutched at her stays. She knew she shouldn't have coaxed Anna to pull them quite so tight—now she could barely breathe. She stopped her headlong flight and leaned against a lamp post, bending at the waist to take deep breaths and hopefully calm the dizziness that threatened to send her into that too-familiar blackness. She knew she fainted too often—Mother always told her so—but if a girl was going to land the most eligible bachelor in New York City, she had to have the smallest waist. And she was determined to do just that.

Her head cleared and she straightened her back, then walked quickly but sedately toward home. Thank goodness she lived only a few city blocks away from Cousin Effie's house. The darkness of evening was quickly falling, and she watched a man coming toward her along the street, lighting lamps as he went.

She was dying to know what all the fuss was about. She loved to hear of others' tribulations, so long as it didn't impact her. And in this case she wasn't sure—that was why she had to get home. She hoped it wouldn't be anything so bad for her poor uncle. Maybe he'd just had a bad day at the office he shared with her father. Yet if that were the case, why was he in such a state? The two brothers had always been close and shared everything, even once courting the same woman, now her mother. She knew Mother had been very beautiful in her youth, and still was—people often remarked on it. It made Della feel plain by comparison.

She pushed open the heavy front door of her house and peered into the parlor. There was no one around, so she followed the hallway to the kitchen. The cook, Mrs. Pippin, looked up at her with a smile. "Good evenin' to ya, Miss Della. Are ya lookin' for someone in particular?"

She nodded. "Yes, Mother. Is she around?"

The cook frowned. "I believe she is, though I hain't seen her for a while. Why don't you try her rooms upstairs?"

Della waved her thanks and hurried off. She passed by the library and found her father there, sitting alone. The smoke from his cigar circled his head in the darkness. She paused. She'd never seen him this way before.

He was usually so jovial, so cheery, that she wasn't sure what to do.

But Mother would know. She left him there and skipped up the stairs two at a time, almost losing her footing on the slick timber. Sally must have waxed the floors. She regained her balance, smoothed her skirts and bustled into her mother's rooms through the slightly ajar door. She too sat in semi-darkness, at her dressing table, brushing her hair slowly and regarding her reflection in the looking glass.

"Mother?" whispered Della, gingerly tiptoeing forward.

Her mother laid the hairbrush on the table and turned in her seat to face her daughter. "Oh, Della, we're ruined."

"What?" Della's brow furrowed. What in Heaven's name did she mean, "ruined"?

Her mother put her face in her hands and began to sob. Della rushed to her side and searched a drawer for a clean handkerchief. She handed it to her mother and knelt beside her, waiting.

Della's mother sat up and pressed the handkerchief to her reddened eyes. "Thank you, my dear."

"Mother, what's happened?"

"A scoundrel, a good for nothing low-life rotten rascal of a man, has swindled your father and uncle out of everything they own. They're in debt too, and as if that wasn't enough he's been spreading the vilest lies about them all over town." She blew her nose loudly into the handkerchief and stood up to pace across the room.

Della stood as well, her hands pressed against her forehead, eyes wide with disbelief. "How can that be?

Father has a good reputation—people know him. They know he wouldn't do anything wrong."

Her mother paused to blow her nose again, then continued pacing, waving her arms around wildly and crying as she did. "It's no use. This man, I don't even know his name, has fixed it so no one will listen to your father's side of the story! He's destroyed us!"

Della's heart fell, and she felt panic rise from her stomach. How could this be? Who would do such a thing? She knew she wouldn't get anything more of use from Mother, so she decided to run back downstairs to see Father. But as she dashed down the long hallway, she heard crying coming from the room her sisters shared. She stopped, pushed their door open and saw them sitting huddled together on a bed, their arms around each other's shoulders and crying. She wondered where her younger brothers were—likely hiding somewhere, or perhaps still playing in the back yard.

She sighed and stepped into the room. "It's going to be all right," she whispered. She sat beside them on the bed and laid a hand on Pearl's shoulder as her youngest sister hiccupped.

Hattie sat straight, sniffled and looked at her through tears. "How do you know?"

"Because Father will work something out. I know he will." She forced a smile, hoping to set her sisters at ease.

It worked—their tears slowed. They sniffled a few more times, then sat still, their faces morose. "What do we do now?" asked Pearl.

"Well, first things first—let's go down and have some supper. Nothing seems quite so bad on a full stomach." Della's voice was brisk and cheery, but her hands trembled as she spoke.

They all stood and walked arm-in-arm down to the dining room, where the aroma of fresh baked rolls and hearty chicken soup wafted out from the kitchen to greet them. Della's stomach growled, and as she sat she noted the fine bone china, silverware and the crystal chandelier that hung over the long table. She frowned. How long would their house look this way? She had no way of knowing, since she still didn't know how much damage the swindler had done. But she did know that her chances of finding a good match with one of New York's most eligible bachelors would dwindle. She'd call on Robert Wilkins first thing in the morning and see about renewing his interest in her.

That decision made, Della felt the fog of despair lift a little. She'd go see Robert, and after their engagement everything would be just fine…for her, at least.

Chapter Two

Della still couldn't believe the hide of Robert Wilkins, Esq. How dare he refuse even to see her when she called on him?

But that was days ago, and now something worse had happened—her mother, against all her pleadings and tears, had sent her and her sisters off to the frontier as mail-order brides! She was to marry some strange man who lived in Montana Territory. She hadn't even known where Montana Territory was—she'd had to look it up in Father's atlas.

How could this be happening? She was supposed to be a debutante enjoying the third year after her coming out. Yes, she'd taken her time choosing a husband, but that was her prerogative, wasn't it? Well, she certainly regretted it now. If she'd been engaged, this whole sordid affair might not have touched her. But now that she no longer had an inheritance of any kind and her family's reputation lay in ruins, none of her old beaus would have her.

She stared bleakly out the window of the steam train as it chugged west along the straight rail lines, every moment taking her further from New York and civilization and closer to the Hades that awaited her. She took a long deep breath, watching a line of rainwater trickle down the windowpane, obscuring her view of the precipitous mountain range she'd spotted to the north a few minutes earlier. It had been a welcome sight after days of endless plains of waving yellow grasses, only broken by the occasional copse of trees.

It had rained nonstop the past several hours and she welcomed it. The sun shouldn't shine when her heart was broken. She didn't know when, or if, she'd ever see her family again—she'd clung to her sisters' necks and they to hers, crying and begging not to be parted. She hadn't even had the chance to say goodbye to Effie or any of her other cousins—Effie had left to meet her new husband in Oregon a few days earlier. Della hoped desperately they'd meet again, but she knew it wasn't likely.

And today she'd meet the man she was to spend the rest of her life with, in the new booming mining town of Livingston. She shuddered at the thought.

The train began to slow, and she grabbed the arm of the seat to steady herself. A loud whistle blasted out over the valley, and she turned to take a look. A small town hurried toward them, spirals of smoke curling skyward from chimneys. It still looked new, with raw timber constructions dotted around and stores and houses being built by the dozen. The rain was falling even harder now and she couldn't see much beyond a few of the closest structures.

They pulled into the small, neat station, and the engine stopped with a groan. She picked up her bonnet from the seat beside her and quickly pinned it onto her head. Then, with her reticule in one hand and her parasol in the other, she stood to her feet and hurried to the door. It opened and a porter grinned at her. "Welcome to Livingston, Miss. Mind yer step." She nodded and gave him her hand to help her down.

As soon as she stood on the platform, she looked up and down the length of it. How would she recognize her future husband? She knew nothing at all about him, except his name—Clement White—and that he was a banker. At least he wasn't a chimney sweep. She frowned at the thought and opened her parasol. The crowds that departed the train milled around the platform, so she pushed through them to stand beneath the station's sturdy tin roof, where the porter had been nice enough to deposit her bags. She thought she'd wait to see who was left after the other travelers dispersed.

Within ten minutes, there was only one man left at the station who didn't wear a railway uniform. He looked like she imagined a cowboy would—long brown dungarees, a checked shirt and a wide-brimmed hat shielding his bearded face. He saw her, his eyes wide, and walked over, holding in his hand a bedraggled bunch of daisies. He touched his fingers to his hat, his face serious. "Della Stout?"

She nodded. "Yes. I'm Della. And you are?"

He held out his hand. "I'm Clement White. It's a pleasure to meet ya, Miss Stout."

She shook his hand quickly, then pulled away. "These are my bags."

While he tried to figure how he could carry all her luggage at once, she looked him up and down beneath hooded eyes. He certainly was handsome, in a dull, country kind of way. He had nothing on the dashing

Robert Wilkins—not that she cared one jot for Robert, after the way he'd treated her.

She followed him dejectedly through the rain along the platform, then down the slippery steps to the muddy street beyond. When she didn't see a cab waiting for them, she shook her head. Was she to slosh through all this mud like a common vagabond? Apparently he expected her to, and she had no choice but to follow him. He was already disappearing across the street, buried beneath a mound of carpetbags and luggage, and didn't turn back to check on her progress. She'd soon lose sight of him if she didn't keep up.

She lifted her skirts high with the same hand that held her reticule and tiptoed through the muck behind him, biting her lip. The least he could have done was order a cab to take her home—now her second-best pair of boots would be ruined. She wondered for a moment when she'd next get a chance to buy a pair of boots. She'd always relied on Father to buy everything she needed—what if her new husband wasn't as generous?

Just thinking of Father and her family brought a lump to her throat, and she choked back the tears. It wouldn't do to cry in front of Clement White…not that he'd be able to tell, since she could already feel the rain soaking through her parasol and running down the sides of her face. Oh, this really was the absolute worst! Her hat was likely ruined, her boots covered in mud, and she was being left to fend for herself through a veritable swamp, past wagons, buggies and men who stopped to watch her as she passed by. The only women around were hovering by the entrances to saloons and dance halls and who knew what else, wearing little more than pantaloons and bustiers. What kind of place had her mother sent her to?

She bit even harder on her lip to stifle the sob that rose in her throat.

Clement White flung the luggage down on the bank floor and let out a huff of breath. How much dang luggage did one half-pint of a woman need? He panted hard, lifting one arm to stretch out his shoulder. But then, he supposed she'd packed up an entire life and moved it across the country. He should give her leave for that.

He glanced over his shoulder as his bride-to-be stumbled in the large oak door and across the timber boards as if drunk. It brought a smirk to his face, but he hid it behind a cough. "Ya all right there?"

She glared at him and dropped her now-useless parasol to the ground. "I most certainly am not."

His eyebrows arched and he lifted the luggage onto his back again. He still had to get it all upstairs to his apartment above the bank. It was cozy and made it easy for him to open and close the bank whenever needed, not to mention to keep an eye on things.

She was looking around the empty building in confusion. "Where are we?"

"This is my bank. We'll be living upstairs. Follow me."

"Where is everyone?"

"I closed up for today." He headed for a door in the back of the room, flung it open and shuffled through, careful not to get wedged in the doorway. With a few grunts and shoves he began struggling up the staircase beyond. When he reached the apartment, he once again relieved himself of the luggage and threw himself into a chair to catch his breath.

Della soon appeared, peering over the top of the staircase, her eyes wide. "What in Heaven's name is this? Is this our *house*?"

He rolled his eyes behind his hand, then managed a smile for her. He could tell just what she thought about it. "Yep, this is where we'll live. I hope it'll be to yer liking."

She frowned as she reached the doorway at the top of the stairs and gazed around, her hands folded demurely in front of her fine black damask gown, white lace framing her neck and wrists. He watched her, noting the long brown loops of hair that no doubt shone in the sunlight when they weren't soaked. Her dainty face had a golden glow, and large hazel eyes absorbed her surroundings before fixing on him. She seemed to be waiting for him to say something.

He cleared his throat and stood quickly. "Well, bedroom's in there if you'd like to get cleaned up. I'll take yer bags in there directly. I can make us a cup of coffee if ya like, 'fore we head on down to see the Reverend." He lifted the first bag and carried it into the small bedroom they'd share. One look at the bed made him gulp. He knew they'd be married before nightfall, but now that she was here, the thought of sharing a bed with her made his breath catch in his throat, and his body break out in a cold sweat, all at the same time.

She followed him. "What do you mean by 'see the Reverend'?"

He lay the bag on the floor and put his hands on his hips. Her head was cocked to one side, and he noticed for the first time how shapely her trim figure was beneath the black silk. "To get hitched, of course. We cain't stay here together without bein' married. I mean, we could, but my Ma raised me better'n that." He felt his cheeks warm beneath her gaze.

"You mean we're getting married…today?"

"'Course. This bed is ours to share. Would ya rather we share it unmarried?"

Her hands flew to cover her mouth. "Well, of course not. It's just that this is all happening so quickly…"

He stepped closer to her and laid a hand on her arm. "Ya came here to marry me, right?"

She nodded.

"So that's what we'll do today. But after that, we can take the rest of it as slow as ya like." He kept his voice soft, feeling a stab of compassion for the young woman. She must be reeling, completely out of her depth, her eyes flitted around the place like a frightened bird. "Unless ya'd rather stay at the hotel on Main Street tonight, 'n we can see the Rev tomorrow."

Her eyes lit up. "Oh, could we do that? I think a good night's sleep is all I really need. I'll be able to face everything much better tomorrow."

"If ya like. I'll take ya there soon as yer ready."

She nodded and drew a deep breath, her round eyes fixed on his. She really was beautiful, and he had to look away lest he steal a kiss before she was ready and scare her further. He walked into the kitchen to wait while she tidied herself. His coat needed a quick brush-down where some of the rain had snuck beneath his overcoat or trickled under the brim of his hat, but otherwise he was ready to go. He'd dressed in his nicest shirt that morning, prepared to look his best for his bride's arrival.

But he'd seen the way she'd appraised him, as though he didn't live up to any of her expectations. Well, if she wanted him to dress differently, she could fix him some new clothes whenever she had a mind to.

The thought occurred to him that perhaps she didn't know how to sew. He could tell from the gown she wore that she came from a family of means, the kind of money he'd never had in his life. No doubt with wealth like that, she'd had people to wait on her, serve her, fix her meals, sew her clothes and good Lord knew what else.

He shook his head. What had he gotten himself into? And why was she here? What had happened to send her away from a family like that? When he'd signed up with the mail-order bridal service, he'd assumed he'd get a wife from a working family, someone sturdy, strong and used to pitching in. Not that there was much for his wife to do in the way of hard work—being a banker certainly had its perks over, say, a dairy farmer. But if they were to have a family of their own, she'd need to be able to run the household, a hard job for even the most robust bride.

He lit the fire in the stove and got it going, filled the coffee pot and set it on a burner to heat. No doubt a cup of something hot would give them both a much-needed boost after their dash through the cold, wet streets of Livingston.

He looked around the room with satisfaction—the small kitchen table, the potbellied stove and chimney, the brick oven, and pots and pans hanging from hooks in the ceiling above the table. The dining area with a card table and two chairs, one of which had a bum leg, kept steady with a piece of kindling. The modest sit-

ting room with a worn love seat and sofa, and brick
fireplace tucked into the wall below a solid mantle
built with his own two hands—a feature he was rather
proud of, given his limited experience in construction.

But now, seeing it through her eyes, he noticed the
chipped woodwork, the peeling paint, the dusty sideboard and the scuffed floor. He gritted his teeth as he
slipped his still-damp hat back on his head. It wasn't
much, but it was all he had and he'd worked dang hard
to get it. Back in Virginia, he'd studied every night
while he was just a lad until he finally landed a job
at a local bank. He'd worked two jobs for years until
he'd saved enough to come west and build this place.

The journey to Montana Territory on the hard seat
of a covered wagon, or more often trudging alongside it, had been lonesome and grueling. He'd almost
died of a fever out on the Nebraska prairie one night,
but thankfully some folks from the wagon train he'd
joined in Oklahoma were there to tend to him and he
pulled through. One day he hoped to have a few acres
of his own, with a sprawling house, stables for his
fine Morgan horses and a barn for a few cattle, hogs
and chickens.

He had big dreams. He'd given up so much, been
through so much, to make it this far. He wasn't about
to let a woman from New York City make him feel bad
about it, even if she was to be his wife.

Just then Della poked her head through the doorway
from the bedroom, then stepped through hesitantly.
She'd changed into a light blue gown, an overcoat was
slung over her arm, a wide-brimmed straw hat on her
head. She almost took his breath away, and he had to

clear his throat. "Would ya like some coffee before we go?"

She dipped her head, her hands clasped shyly in front of her. He poured them each a cup of thick black chicory coffee, and her eyes widened as he handed her the cup. "Thank you," she whispered, then, "I suppose I'll have to learn how to do that."

He frowned, took a sip of coffee and let the hot liquid slip down his throat and warm his belly. "Hmmm… do what?"

"Make coffee," she said matter-of-factly.

He started, his eyebrows arching. "You've never made coffee."

She shook her head and took a dainty sip.

"Have you built a fire before?"

Again she shook her head.

He took a deep breath. It was worse than he'd thought.

Della's nose wrinkled and she pursed her lips. So much for the idea of staying at the hotel—one look at it and she'd hidden behind Clem's back, darting looks over his shoulder at the raucous scene. There was no way she'd stay there if she had any other choice. Sporting women spilled out of its doors, a tinny piano played a bawdy melody, and the sounds, sights and smells that emanated from its depths were more than she could stomach. "*This* is where you want me to stay?" she'd cried.

He'd chuckled and said it was all they had in town. But if she'd rather, they could go down to the church and get married now. She'd reluctantly nodded, and he'd escorted her to the quaint white building with the steeple on the edge of town. She'd rather take her chances marrying a stranger. At least his little apartment above the bank wasn't brimming with scantily clad women and drunken louts.

Reverend Holstead was a tall, skinny man with a few straggly strands of hair combed over his round, bald pate. He peered down at her over the tops of his spectacles and recited their vows in a monotone while his wife stood by with her hands clasped together and her face pulled into a wide smile. The ceremony was over before she knew it, and she'd barely heard a word, though her own responses seemed to satisfy the group. Then her new husband set her overcoat around her shoulders, shrugged into his own and dragged her off through the pelting rain back to the bank.

The brevity of the ceremony made her want to weep. But she held in the tears, along with her breath, and vowed to think about it another day—some time when she could stomach it.

As she shook yet another coating of mud from her boots, she considered how glad she was that she hadn't changed shoes earlier, else two pairs would be ruined. Were any of the roads in this miserable place paved, or would she spend the rest of her life trudging through mud and dust?

Chapter Three

Della lay as close to the edge of the bed as she could. It was warm beneath the covers, but still she trembled. She hadn't gotten much sleep during her first night sharing a bed with her new husband. All night long she'd been acutely aware of the man lying only inches away from her, breathing deeply in his slumber.

He stirred beside her, then swung his feet over the edge of the bed and rubbed his eyes, but she lay still, pretending to be asleep. She couldn't help it—she knew they were married now and he was her husband and it made no sense at all for her to be afraid of him. But still, she'd just met him.

He dressed quickly, and she heard the clomp of his boots on the staircase as he descended. Within moments, all was quiet in the apartment—he must have gone down to work. What should she do with him gone?

She sat up straight, rubbed the sleep from her eyes and stood to her feet with a yawn. She hoped she'd learn to sleep beside him soon, or before long she'd be so exhausted she wouldn't be able to think straight.

Stumbling into the kitchen, she studied the stove and saw he hadn't lit it. She would really love some hot coffee and perhaps a croissant. But one of those was not to be—a quick search of the kitchen table, pantry and drawers revealed half a loaf of bread, some cheese wrapped in a cloth, a dozen potatoes and a few apples. No croissants in sight. She did, however, find a pitcher of cream with a towel laid over it and some coffee. Now she just had to figure out how to heat it.

She eyed the stove and tugged a small knob on the door. It opened and she saw the ash from the previous day inside. There was a stack of firewood beside the stove, so she shoved a couple of pieces in, found the flint in a small dish nearby, and squealed with glee when it sent sparks onto the firewood with her first try. But it didn't take and the flame soon died away. She frowned and stood looking at it with one hand on her hip, tapping her chin with a finger. What had she done wrong? She'd seen fires lit a million times before—why couldn't she do it herself?

She added a few smaller pieces of kindling, tried again, and this time they caught. Soon she had quite a blaze going and, grinning with pride over her small achievement, she put the coffee pot on and waited for it to boil. In ten minutes she had a steaming cup of weak coffee between her hands and was sipping it gingerly, careful not to burn her lips.

Once she finished the cup, she cleaned up after herself, then washed and dressed. She sat on the love seat in the sitting room, drummed her fingers on her knees a few times, then stood and wandered to the window to peer out at the street below. The sun had decided to show itself, and the street bustled with activity. Women hurried along the boardwalk or rode by in wagons. Men skipped across the street, minding the buggies and riders as they went.

It was so very different to what she was used to. The streets were nothing but mud after several days of rain, and the muck caught on everything it touched—wheels, boots, dress hems. The people scurried around dressed in blacks and browns, Stetsons and bonnets, nothing fashionable, all practical. She knew if she stepped outside, she'd stand out like a sore thumb in her emerald satin gown with black stripes and matching doll hat with its regal cockade of feathers.

She wrinkled her nose. But if she didn't go out, what *would* she do while Clement was at work? Perhaps she should go downstairs and see what he was up to. She wrapped a shawl around her shoulders, almost grabbed her parasol from where she'd leaned it against the banister before deciding it would be a bit too much, and hurried down the staircase.

The bank was bright and sunny, and a man with a holstered revolver lounged by the front door. There were three tellers at their windows, and behind them was a small office—Clement's, she presumed. The door was closed and she stood still for a few moments, twisting her hands together. But in a minute, the office door swung open and she saw Clement, dressed in another checked shirt but missing the hat, stride out with a young couple. The woman smiled nervously at him and the man shook his hand, then they turned and left.

Clement saw Della, waved to her, and her heart jumped. She smiled and waved back. He marched over and took her hand in his. "Good mornin'," he said with a grin. "Didja sleep well?"

She nodded. Her skin tingled at his touch and her cheeks flushed with warmth. "Fine," she lied.

"Sorry I didn't talk to ya this mornin', but I didn't wanna wake ya 'n I had to get to work." He still held her hand between his, and she wondered when he'd release it. Still, she liked the warm feeling of it.

"Of course, I understand. It's just…"

"Just what?"

"What should I do with myself?"

He tipped his head to one side and his eyes crinkled at the corners. "What do ya mean?"

"While you're working, what should I do all day?"

"How did you spend your time back in New York?" he asked, releasing her hand and scratching his head.

She felt a stab of disappointment that he'd let go, and took a deep breath. "I spent time with friends, with my sisters and cousins. I did needlepoint, I played piano… I was learning French—my tutor came once a week for that. And I'd go to shows, soirees, parties. I'd dance, or go on picnics with friends. There was always something to do…" She paused as the memories flooded her mind and made her mood drift downward.

He frowned. "Well…we ain't got any French tutors here, though I'm sure ya could find a few Frenchies to talk to when they're not down in the mines. I can look into gettin' a piano if ya like—not sure where I'd find one, but I'll ask around…"

She shook her head. "Never mind. I never really liked it much anyway."

"You could take a walk, have a look around," he said with a wry smile. "But first, lemme introduce ya…" He led her to where the first teller sat at a window protected by vertical iron bars. The woman wore a slim-fitting dress with a colorful scarf around her neck. She had luxurious mahogany hair, and her pouting lips parted to reveal brilliantly white teeth. "Della, I'd like ya to meet Francisca Schmidt, one of my tellers. I'm sure the two of ya'll will get along just fine."

Della shook Francisca's hand and gave her a well-practiced smile. "A pleasure to meet you."

"And you too," replied the woman in a soft accent. "Welcome to Livingston," she answered precisely. "How do you like it so far?"

Della blushed. "Well, I can't say—I haven't seen much of it. But it's certainly different from what I'm used to."

Francisca nodded. "*Si*, I imagine it is. Perhaps you'd like to join my Bible study group. It might make it easier to make friends here."

"Oh yes, well…"

"I know, it does not sound very exciting—you are probably used to many exciting parties and balls where you are from. But here in Livingston, unless you like to gamble or drink in a dance hall, better to settle for a quiet group. We meet each week at my house."

"Thank you." Della glanced up at Clement, who nodded his encouragement. "That sounds lovely."

Della's boot stuck in the mud when she crossed the street. She yanked it free before a buggy sailed past, narrowly missing her. The driver shouted and shook his fist at her, and she waved an apology as she hobbled to the boardwalk. She wiped her boot clean on the edge of a board and set off again.

The clang of a blacksmith's tools filled the air, and she snuck a look inside a wooden building to watch a man hammering a red-hot horseshoe into shape. She passed a mercantile, and made a mental note to stop in on her way back to see what products they sold. She didn't hold out much hope for their selection, but perhaps she'd find a few things she needed. Then she saw a sign hanging from a shop front ahead: *The Lucky Emerald.* She frowned. What type of establishment could it be? She thought it unlikely she'd find a fine jeweler's in Livingston, Montana Territory.

She stepped forward, ready to sneak a look inside, when a woman rushed past, knocking her to the ground. She fell on her hands and knees with a cry. The woman had been short and broad, wearing a worn gray dress with matching bonnet—and carrying an axe!

With a gasp, Della leaped to her feet and looked toward the swinging double doors the woman disappeared through. She heard shouts and cries from within, and pushed cautiously inside what looked to be a saloon. The woman was swinging her axe with great heaves into the bar, chopping it into kindling. A man ducked around her, shouting and clutching at his dingy bowler hat with both hands. "C'mon now, Honey, give it up or I'm callin' the sheriff on ya! You're gonna destroy my bar!"

Della's eyes widened and she froze in place.

The woman turned on the barkeeper with a snarl. "This place! You take a man's hard-earned money— that's food right out of his family's mouth, you know it is! But do you care? No, you don't care one jot! Well, let's see how you like it when the tables turn!" She swung the axe down hard, splitting the bar. The axe stuck in place and she tugged hard on it but couldn't budge it.

The man grabbed her from behind and twisted her arm up behind her back, making her squeal. "Joe comes in here of his own accord—I don't make him spend that money. Now, let's go see the sheriff. Ya can't just come in here and do this whenever ya get angry at yer husband. Why don'tcha try talkin' to *him* about it sometime?" His tone was sympathetic, even as he shoved her ahead of him past Della, out the doors and down the street.

Della ran a hand over her face and took a deep breath. Her legs trembled and the street began to sway. She tried to keep breathing, but felt as though she couldn't. Oh dear, why couldn't the floor stay still for a moment so she could get her bearings? She really should stop wearing her stays so tight—and anyway, it couldn't possibly matter what size her waist was any longer. She reached out both hands, stumbled backward out the doors and fell, landing with a thud and knocking her head hard on the timber boards.

Just then, two strong arms slipped around her, lifting her from the ground. She glanced up to see Clement's brown eyes hovering over hers, his brows drawn low and his forehead creased with concern. "Della?"

Then she closed her eyes and drifted off.

Chapter Four

The room was dark when Della woke, and it took her a few moments to figure out where she was. She sat up and grabbed her head with a groan. With her fingers, she gently palpated the back of her skull to discover a large, painful lump. She rubbed it ruefully, then swung her legs over to rest her feet on the floor.

She was in the bedroom of the apartment, and the curtains had been pulled shut across the window. There was no way of knowing what time of day it was, though she could see the glow of sunshine from behind the fabric. The sound of footsteps outside pricked her ears and she stood slowly, smoothing her hair back into place with both hands.

When she peeked through the cracked-open doorway, she saw Clement sitting on the love seat, his legs crossed leisurely, sipping a cup of coffee and reading a newspaper. Spectacles perched on the end of his nose, and furrows creased his forehead. He looked up, half-grinned and slipped his spectacles off, placing them on the table beside him. "Ya up?"

She nodded. "Thank you for helping me. I must have hit my head." Again she patted the lump and winced.

"Ya sure did." He stood and hurried to her side, offering her his arm for support as he led her to the kitchen table and helped her take a seat. "Coffee comin' right up!"

"Thank you."

She watched him fill a cup. Then he sliced a thick piece of bread onto a plate, and slathered it with creamy butter and a spoonful of preserves. He'd rolled up his shirt sleeves, and his biceps and forearms bulged when he bent his arms. His pants fitted tightly around his muscular thighs and trim waist. She blushed—she hadn't noticed before just how attractive he was—and her face heated up as though she were sitting by a fire. She fanned herself with one hand and sighed. Heaven's above, how hard had she hit her head? She must be hallucinating if watching a cowboy banker serve her a slice of bread made her pulse race.

He strode back to the table and lay the snack in front of her, then watched as she took a sip, his hands on his hips. She glanced up at him under arched eyebrows. "I'm fine, really—no need to hover, I assure you. Just a little bump on the head, nothing to worry about. Come to mention it, though, who was that woman? She was a menace! She might have killed me if I'd been there a few seconds earlier."

He laughed and took a seat beside her. "That was Honey Barnes. And no, she wouldn't have killed ya or anyone else. She's just fired up 'cause her husband Joseph went and drank away his wages again. She does it every now and then. Hank Welch the saloon owner gets bent out of shape 'bout the damage she does, but he's too tender-hearted to press charges, and thanks to Joe she ain't got the money to pay for it anyhow. So she spends the night in the sheriff's lockup, then they take her home once she's calmed down."

Della's eyes widened as his story progressed. "How often does she do this?"

"'Bout every six months or so."

Della took another sip and pondered his words. What a strange place this was, where a woman could deface an establishment with an axe and be sent home, only to do it all over again a few months later. "What time is it?"

"Oh, 'bout five o'clock. I let Francisca and Jim close up the bank for me today so I could sit here with ya."

She ducked her head. "I'm so sorry. I hope I didn't cost you any business."

"No, no. Yer my priority now." He grinned and popped his spectacles back on his nose. "I'm afraid ya'll think me an old fuddy-duddy with these things on my face, but I cain't read without 'em."

"Not at all," she said, but admitted to herself he didn't look quite the same. Not worse, just different— smarter, perhaps.

He smiled. "Did ya wanna try out that women's Bible study group?"

"Well…"

"I will admit, most of the women in this town don't seem to me the kind ya'd likely strike up a friendship with. The Bible study group is a higher class of social gathering for women, accordin' to my understandin'. It might be good for ya—ya could make some friends. It'd help ya get settled, I reckon."

She chewed her lower lip in thought. Really, all she

wanted to do was go back to bed, curl up in a ball and lay in the dark. She didn't want to meet anyone. Her head hurt, she missed home and she was beginning to fully appreciate just how much her life had changed in the past few weeks. Nothing would be the same for her ever again. But, perhaps he was right—if this was to be her life from now on, it made sense for her to try and find some friends to share that life with. It might make things a bit easier for her, though after meeting a few of the locals she highly doubted it. If only Effie or Hattie or Pearl had come to the same town, she might have been able to stand it all. "I suppose I can go once, try it out. When is it?"

"Tonight after supper." His eyes drifted back to the sitting room and his newspaper. "What're we havin'?"

Her eyes flew wide. Was he suggesting she should cook for them?

Francisca and Hans Schmidt owned a tiny cottage built from rough-cut lumber covered in tar paper, with shingles for the roof. It could have looked worse, but Francisca had a talent for home decoration—inside the house it fairly glowed with cozy warmth and love. Colorful rugs lit up every floor surface, lace curtains lined the windows and fresh flowers stood in vases on every flat surface. There were works of art on the walls, and the basic furniture was adorned with lovingly crafted pillows and bric-a-brac. "Your home is lovely," said Della, untying her hat and putting it on the coat rack with her coat.

"Oh, thank you so much," sighed Francisca, taking her by the arm and leading her into the den. "Come and meet everybody. I am so glad you are here. I was worried about you today when *Señor* White carried you in after you hurt your head. You were so pale! I told him he should get the doctor, but he was sure you would be fine. And here you are!"

"I feel much better, though my head still hurts a bit." Della entered the room, and everybody turned to watch her.

"Everyone, this is Della White," announced Francisca proudly. "She is from New York City!"

The dozen women smiled and murmured welcomes. Most immediately turned back to their conversations, but one caught her eye and waved. She lifted her hand awkwardly to return the gesture, then noticed another lady standing by a punch bowl, dipping her cup in and lifting it tentatively to her lips. She had wavy auburn hair, full lips, brown eyes and curves that filled out her fitted blue dress…

Della gasped and spun away, her face pale. It was the woman from the saloon, Honey.

"What is it, dear?" asked Francisca, her brow furrowed.

"That woman is here—the axe-wielding madwoman from the saloon who almost killed me!" she whispered, shooting looks over her shoulder to make sure she wasn't about to be attacked again.

Francisca's face relaxed, and she chuckled in amusement. "Oh, you mean Honey? No, she is perfectly safe. Honey—come over and meet your latest victim!"

Della blanched, and grabbed hold of Francisca's forearm. "No, no," she hissed. She turned slowly to find herself face to face with Honey.

Honey's eyebrows arched high, her cheeks flushed

red. "Victim? Oh dear, what have I done now?" she asked, concern in her melodic voice.

Della forced herself to smile.

Francesca pried her arm free and rubbed it with relief. "Now, now, Della, no need to be afraid. Honey would not hurt a fly—intentionally."

"No, I certainly wouldn't."

"Well, you just about killed me today," snapped Della, her heart pounding. "You knocked me down in front of that saloon you chopped to pieces."

Honey looked ashamed, covering her mouth with her hand. "Oh, that was you? I'm so sorry—I didn't see you there, and I was intent on finding that scoundrel Hank. I hope you weren't hurt."

Della felt pity at the look of horror on the young woman's face. "Never mind. I suppose all's well that ends well. I did get an awful bump on the back of my head, but I'll live."

Honey grabbed her hands and took them between hers, squeezing them tight. "I hope you can forgive me."

"Well, I suppose…"

"It's just that sometimes I can't take it anymore. Joe drank it all away, again, and the children are hungry. Francisca here and Abella help out when they can, but it's just not enough when you've got so many little mouths to feed. Not to mention they all need new boots and clothes. I just don't know sometimes how we're gonna make it. I come here every week in the hopes that if we all pray about it together, maybe something will change."

Della's chest tightened. No wonder the poor woman

had just about gone mad. "How many children do you have?"

"Five so far. I've told Joe no more, but he pays no mind to anything I say, and I seem to be as fertile as a deer mouse." She snorted.

Francisca patted Honey's arm. "There, there—let us not worry about what has not happened yet. Each of your little ones is as precious as anyone could be."

Honey nodded sadly. "I know. Sometimes they drive me to distraction so I forget, but they are precious."

Francisca turned to the group. "Shall we begin, ladies?"

Everyone ended their conversations and made their way to the various sofas, armchairs and stools scattered around Francisca's small den. Francisca hurried to the kitchen and came back wearing an apron and carrying a tray of food. Another lady, a blonde with her hair in a high bun, followed with a tray full of tea cups and a teapot in a cunning knitted cozy. She smiled warmly and chatted easily with the women around her. "Help yourselves," encouraged Francisca, passing cups around the group, as the women pulled out their Bibles, and began their discussion on the book of Esther.

Della took a seat beside Honey, who grabbed a small sandwich and shoved it indelicately into her mouth.

She leaned over toward Honey and whispered into her ear. "Francisca is so exotic-looking and has such an interesting accent. Do you know where she's from?"

"Oh yes, she's from Chile. She traveled from there to Seattle on a steamboat." Honey took another sandwich and gulped it down.

Della wondered how often the poor woman got to

eat a hearty meal. "Oh, how interesting. And who's the blonde lady with Francisca?"

Honey finished chewing and swallowed nervously, patting her mouth with a napkin. "Abella Goode—she's Francisca's best friend."

Della nodded and crossed her ankles demurely. "Well, she's very pretty."

"She sure is. She was a soiled dove, you know."

Della gasped, her eyes bulging. "What?"

"Yep. Came all the way from France, and her husband went and died on her, out on the Oregon Trail. When she got to Livingston, she had to take a job as a sporting woman just to get a roof over her head and a meal in her belly. Back then, there weren't many jobs for anyone, let alone a Frenchwoman on her own. But then Stanley Goode—an Englishman, mind you—fell in love with her and asked her to marry him. Ever since, she's been trying to work her way into the proper circles, but none of these women'll have anything to do with her."

Della watched Abella move gracefully around the group, offering the plate of treats to each woman in turn, and noticed the subtle ways each of them snubbed her, something that had escaped her attention before: a turning away of the head, pretending not to hear her, excluding her from their conversations or acting as though their cup of tea absorbed all their attention. But still, Abella smiled and acted as though nothing was amiss.

Soon she reached Della and Honey and offered them the tray. "Would you ladies like something to eat?" she asked. Her blue eyes sparkled, and Della saw tiny freckles sprinkled across her dainty nose.

"Yes, please!" said Honey, grabbing a handful of sandwiches.

"Thank you." Della reached for a sandwich and a napkin.

"You must be Della." Abella's soft French accent made every word sound like a melody.

"Yes, that's right. Della White—I'm pleased to meet you. Honey tells me your name is Abella—what a pretty name." Della refused to treat the poor woman with anything but good manners. After all, her situation wasn't so far removed from the Frenchwoman's. The only difference was that she'd been fortunate enough to be taken in by a kind-hearted man. Her heart thudded at the realization of just what Clement had done for her—and where she might have been if not for him.

Abella's eyes glistened and she inclined her head. "Thank you. That is so kind of you."

The Bible study itself was brief, followed by further conversation and socializing. Della spoke more with Honey and Abella, and the three of them stayed behind to help Francisca clean up. Finally Clement showed up to walk Della home, she saw him standing out on the porch. She wrapped her shawl around her shoulders, tied on her bonnet and waved farewell to her new friends.

Clem leaned against the porch railing waiting for Della. He held his hat in one hand and ran the other through his wild hair, accidentally standing it on end. He hoped for her sake she'd made some friends that evening. He didn't know too much about womenfolk, but he did know they set a whole lot of store on friendships and social circles.

For him, settling into life in Livingston had simply meant working hard day and night until he'd established his business and built the apartment overhead to sleep in. He'd never given a whole lot of thought to relationships, though some had developed naturally over time. He didn't go out of his way to spend time with his friends, just saw them when they came into the bank or went out hunting together. Sometimes he'd go to a church picnic or some other outing, but otherwise he entertained himself with his work. That had kept him well occupied and content for several years. It had only been in the past year that he'd begun to feel something was missing from his life, and when Stan Goode suggested he needed a wife, the idea had taken root and he'd finally written away for a mail-order bride.

He walked behind Della up the stairs to their apartment. She chattered away about the friends she'd made, seeming more chipper after the evening's affair. He smiled in satisfaction. It'd been a good idea after all—he was glad he'd encouraged her to go.

After she'd washed up and changed for bed, he knocked on their bedroom door and entered the darkened room, only to trip over the boots she'd left lying on the floor. She seemed to already have fallen to sleep beneath the covers on her side, facing away from him. He undressed and slipped quickly into his side of the bed. The steady rhythm of her breathing made his skin tingle all over, and he longed to reach out and touch her.

He heard a sob and frowned. Then another, followed by a sniffle. Was she crying? What should he do? It was clear she didn't intend for him to hear her distress—her head was buried in her pillow, muffling the sounds. He tucked his hands under his head, lying still in the darkness listening to her, his heart thumping in his chest. Finally he turned onto his side and laid a hand on her back. "Della? Ya all right?"

She didn't respond, only took a deep breath.

"Della?"

When there was still no response again, he rubbed her back gently, then turned away to give her privacy. He felt completely helpless. He'd thought she'd had a good time at the Bible study, yet here she was crying herself to sleep beside him. He knew then he was in over his head.

Chapter Five

Della peered into the stove, then shut the door with a bang. The fire within was steady, and she'd set the coffee pot on the stove top to boil. So far, so good. She frowned and reached for the handle—perhaps she should move it a little to the left...*ouch!* She pulled her hand back with a gasp and sucked on her fingertips where they'd been burned. Now what? She'd lifted the coffee pot with a cloth the last time, but the cloth was nowhere to be seen. She gathered the edges of her apron around her hand and tried again. There, that was better. She smiled with satisfaction, then looked around for the honey to apply to the burn. Clem had brought some home the previous evening after work, much to her delight. She loved honey, and missed the sweet treats she'd been used to back home.

Clem strode into the room, his face freshly washed and his damp hair combed back from his handsome face. When he smiled, a little dimple crinkled one cheek and made her pulse race. Whenever he came near her now, she tingled all over, and his presence made her nervous. "Good mornin', wife," he said with a chuckle. "And what, pray tell, are ya up to?"

"I'm making coffee," she announced proudly.

"Well, how about that?" He sat at the table and set his hat on one knee.

"Would you like some?"

"Sure would. And is there anythin' to eat?" He arched an eyebrow, looking hopeful.

"Well, I think there's some leftover bread in the bread box. We ate all of the preserves, but..." She stammered, uncertain of what else to say. "What do you usually eat for breakfast? Back in New York, I'd have a croissant with a mug of chocolate or coffee, but I haven't been able to find croissants here."

He frowned. "Well, let's see. I suppose I'd love some pancakes, or cornbread with buttermilk. My Ma used to make oatcakes for me sometimes."

Her cheeks warmed, and she absently sucked the honey from her fingertips. "I see. Where would I find those kinds of things, do you think?"

He tipped his head to one side and stared at her in puzzlement. "Well, ya'd make 'em, of course."

She laughed. "Me? I'm sorry, but you know I don't know how to cook."

He looked miffed at her words and leaned forward in his seat. "I'm sure it ain't that hard."

She was getting more flustered by the moment. What did he expect from her? Was she to be his servant now, waiting on him hand and foot? It all seemed too much for her to bear—she didn't know the first thing about how to make an oatcake, pancake, or any other cake for that matter. "What do people around here do for food?" she asked, filling a cup with coffee and handing it to him.

"Well, a lotta men go down to the saloon or the hotel. There's a restaurant 'round the corner, but it's pretty expensive to eat there too often. I dunno... I guess a lot of men just eat beans from a can or johnny-cakes with butter most of the time. That's why we're all so skinny." He chuckled and ran his fingers through his almost-dry hair, then gulped down his coffee.

"I bet if someone opened a café selling home-cooked meals, they'd make a killing here," said Della with a laugh. "I'd sure appreciate it, anyway."

He sighed. "I suppose it's too much to hope for more'n a stale piece of bread for breakfast, then?"

"I'm afraid so." She smiled ruefully, twisted her fingers together in front of her apron—and jumped at the pain of the burn, cradling her sore fingers.

"Well, I'm gonna head down to the mercantile," he grumbled. "Sometimes they got some baked goods there in the mornin'—maybe I'll find somethin' to eat." He stood and slapped his hat onto his head.

Della felt downcast that she hadn't lived up to his expectations, no matter how unreasonable they seemed. "I'm sorry."

He stepped toward her and lifted a hand to trace the outline of her cheek. "Never mind—I'll live," he whispered with a smile. He tucked a strand of hair behind her ear and bent to kiss her on the cheek. Her skin tingled beneath his lips, and she trembled at the look in his brown eyes. With a deep breath, she followed him to the staircase and waved goodbye.

Now what should I do? She remembered Honey saying she accompanied her children to school every morning, and decided to walk in that direction in hope she might run into the woman. She'd been scared half to death by her on their first meeting, but since then she'd grown to like her. And she knew Honey appreciated the friendship, given her troubles at home. She donned a bonnet and headed out through the bank, waving to Francisca and being careful not to disturb Tobias the guard, who looked as though he was dozing.

Outside, the brilliant sunshine blazed down on her, warming her immediately. The mud had dried and now the ground was hard and lumpy. She stepped over a pile of horse manure and around what looked like the remains of someone's half-digested meal, and grimaced. This town needed a department of sanitation, she thought.

The schoolhouse was a small white building with a quaint bell tower above the porch. The ringing of the bell each morning to call the children to class could be heard all over Livingston. She'd resented it the first few mornings it had woken her. Back home, there were always parties and events to attend until well after midnight—she'd sleep in late the next day and take breakfast on a tray in her bedroom. But now, her routine had already changed—she woke early to fix Clem his morning coffee and usually went to bed just after supper. She sighed, remembering the sunlight streaming through the window and Sally lighting a fire in the hearth for her so she wouldn't shiver when she dressed.

Children huddled around the front of the school, making their way up the stairs and inside. She saw Honey immediately, her legs encased in a small boy's eager arms. He looked about five years old and seemed determined not to follow his siblings in, until Honey gave him a kiss and whispered something into his ear. He nodded, released her legs and trudged miserably up the stairs, glancing back over his shoulder at his mother at intervals.

Honey waved goodbye, turned to head home and almost ran into Della, converting her momentum into an embrace at the last second. "Della, how are you?" she cried.

Della's cheeks warmed and her heart leaped. She usually felt so alone with Clem at work most of the time. It was nice to know she was making friends in her new hometown, however unlikely they might be. "I'm fine, I suppose. How about you?"

"Well, Joe's feeling sorry for his behavior, so he's on the water wagon at the moment. It goes in cycles— I'm just enjoying it for now. I really do love the lout— at least when he's sober." She looped her arm through Della's and the two women walked down the street. "So what's wrong? Why are you only fine?"

Della's mouth twisted. "I can't seem to do anything right—well, not in Clem's eyes. It's been so difficult for me, losing everyone and everything in my life. I moved across the country and had to adjust to…well, every-thing! And now he expects me to cook for him, though he knows I don't know how. I was proud of myself for figuring out how to light a fire in the stove and heat up his morning coffee, but now he's asking for pancakes and oatcakes and…" She sighed, her brow furrowed.

Honey laughed. "Most men do expect their wives to cook them a hot breakfast—that's a fact. But don't you worry about it—I'm a good cook if I do say so myself. I can teach you a few things. What are you doing right now?"

Della's eyes widened and she turned to Honey with a grin. "Do you mean it? Really? Oh, that would be wonderful. I'm not doing anything right now."

"Fine, then—let's go to the mercantile, get some supplies and head over to my place for a cooking lesson. What do you say?"

Della nodded vigorously and threw her arms around Honey, squeezing her tight.

Honey laughed. "Whoa, you'll strangle the breath right out of me!"

"Sorry," said Della, pulling away. "I'm just so grateful." Then she frowned. "But I don't want to cost you. I know you're…well, you have a lot of hungry mouths to feed."

"Never mind that," Honey said with a grin. "We'll charge it to your husband's account. With the meal he'll be getting tonight, he won't mind a bit."

By the time the two women finished fixing supper for Della to take home with her, she was covered in a fine coating of flour, had a smear of pie filling across one cheek and her face was a bright shade of red from the heat of the oven that dominated Honey's small kitchen. And she hadn't felt that happy in weeks.

Since Honey was teaching Della all the cooking basics she could in their few hours together, Della had decided she might as well make extra for Honey to feed her own family that night and sell to the neighbors for a bit of cash. It was the only way she could think of to thank Honey for her efforts, since she didn't have money of her own. She decided she'd have to speak with Clem about an allowance, since it had pained her not to be able to give Honey anything other than a few ingredients. She beamed as she lifted the casserole dish filled with venison and potato stew into her hands, then stacked a huckleberry pie on top of it. Honey set a butter cake on the pie, and Della wrapped the lot in a dish towel, hugging it against her body. "This looks wonderful, Honey—I can't thank you enough."

"You're most welcome, my dear. I hope you'll both enjoy it." Honey took a cloth and wiped the smear of huckleberry compote from Della's cheek.

Della laughed. "You know, I tasted a little here and there, and your food is absolutely delicious. Clem told me last night that most of the men in town go hungry for a lack of good home-cooked meals. You could probably make a fortune selling food like this—so many men are here without a wife and family."

Honey's brow furrowed and she put her hands on her plump hips. "Do you think so?"

"I do. You should consider it. It might give you a chance to make a bit of money of your own, so you're not always relying on…well, you know." Della blushed. She hated to criticize another woman's husband, even if he did deserve it.

Honey chewed her cheek thoughtfully. "You may be right. I'll think about it."

"Well, I'd best get going before Clem finishes work, or he'll be wondering where on Earth I am." Della grinned and stepped through Honey's front door and onto the street. A buggy trotted by and the afternoon breeze lifted her hair to fly around her face and blow dust into her eyes. "Oh dear, it's either mud or dust in this town," she said with a grimace.

"That's the truth!" Honey laughed. "See you later, Della my dear. The children will be home from school any moment. I'm glad we made those extra cakes and cookies—they'll think Christmas has come early when they see all the good food in our kitchen." She ducked her head, then whispered with tears in her wide brown eyes. "It's been quite a while since they've seen such a bounty, so really it's *you* I have to thank."

Della smiled and nodded goodbye, unable to speak. It didn't matter how much money there was in the world, she decided, there was nothing more satisfying than helping a friend in need.

When she reached home, she climbed the stairs to the apartment and set the food on the kitchen table with a sigh. She shook her arms and hands with relief—they'd cramped up under the weight halfway home and she'd feared she'd drop the lot right there on Main Street. Only the memory of how much hard work they'd put into fixing it gave her the resolve to ignore the pain and keep trudging onward.

She opened some windows to air out the stuffy room, chastising herself for not thinking of it before she'd left home that morning, then stashed the food in the small pantry and collapsed on the bed with her arms splayed out across the mattress. She'd just lay here a bit to recover—she couldn't remember working so hard in her life before. Every muscle ached, her back hurt, her feet throbbed and she had a horrible headache, her eyeballs seeming to pulse with every heartbeat. She lifted a hand to wipe her forehead, then let it collapse back on the bed with a cry—it seemed every little movement caused her pain. She let out a long breath and closed her eyes.

When she next opened them, the room was dark. She sat up in fright and glanced around—what time was it? A sound beside the bed caught her ear, and she turned to find Clem sitting on a rocking chair on the other side of the bed, puffing on his pipe in the darkness. "Clem?" she asked, rubbing her eyes with her knuckles.

"Yeah, it's me."

"What are you doing?"

"Just sitting. I wanted to make sure yer all right, but didn't wanna wake you." He let out a long stream of smoke and it floated through the air.

She jumped to her feet and smoothed her hair and skirts with her hands. "How long have you been here?"

"Oh, only a few minutes. Don't fret, it ain't that late."

"I'm sorry, I didn't mean to fall asleep like that. I wanted to greet you when you came home." She bustled out of the room.

Clem followed close behind her and sat at the kitchen table. "Never mind—yer doin' it now. Should we go to the hotel for supper?"

She shook her head and grinned. "No need. I made supper."

He half-smiled in surprise, his eyebrows arching. "Ya did what?"

"You heard me." She tied an apron around her waist and retrieved the food, one item at a time, from the pantry, setting it all on the table in front of him. "We have venison and potato stew, huckleberry pie and butter cake."

His head jerked back as he laughed. "Is that so? Now where in tarnation didja learn to do that?"

She pretended to be peeved by his question. "If you must know, at the Barnes'. I went over there today and

Honey showed me how to cook a few things. I hope to go back again sometime and learn more. This is what we made, along with a meal for her family and a few other things." Suddenly she felt her heart lurch. "Um… I charged it all to your account at the mercantile. I hope you don't mind."

He shook his head. "Not at all—that's why I got an account there, so ya can get whatever ya need. And if all this tastes as amazin' as it looks and smells, it's well worth the expense."

Her entire body flooded with warmth under his praises. "Well, let me get you a plate then." She reheated the stew and ladled out two bowls while he washed up in the bedroom. She'd sampled it at Honey's and it seemed delicious to her, but perhaps Clem didn't like venison stew. She'd soon find out.

They held hands while he said the blessing, and again a thrill ran through her at his touch. It was so familiar yet strange to hold hands with this man she'd just begun to get to know. Her family had never held hands to say grace, always bowing their heads over linked fingers. She liked it—it made her feel closer to him somehow.

He concluded, dipped his spoon into the stew, took an enormous bite—and his eyes widened in surprise. Once he swallowed, he exclaimed, "Whoa! Della, I do believe this is now my favorite dish."

Her heart swelled and tears filled the corners of her eyes. She dashed them away with the back of her hand and smiled. A few weeks ago she'd never have believed she could pull off preparing an entire delicious meal. With help, of course, but Honey had insisted she do it herself, only overseeing the work. She felt a surge of pride for overcoming yet another obstacle. Perhaps she was stronger than she'd ever believed herself to be.

Chapter Six

Della stared at the kitchen in dismay. Dirty dishes filled the sink, and every piece of silverware they owned was coffee-stained or encrusted with old food.

Honey, Francisca and Abella had just arrived, calling on her right before noon. The three women had sat in the living room with a direct view into the kitchen and hadn't said a word about the disarray, but Della was embarrassed just the same. She knew she should offer the women something to drink and probably even a bite of lunch, but she didn't have a clean cup or plate to serve it with. Francisca had even had to move a pile of Della's soiled dresses from the settee before she sat down, shifting it to the floor.

A cockroach scuttled across the pile of dirty dishes, and Della screamed.

The three visitors rushed into the kitchen to see what was the matter. Abella grabbed a frying pan out of the sink and held it above her head, ready to mete out punishment to whoever had attacked her friend.

Della pointed at the cockroach and yelled again, backing as far away as the kitchen wall would allow her to flee. Francisca and Honey joined in with screeches of their own and scrambled back away from the creature.

Abella just laughed and brought the frying pan down on the insect, squashing it in one quick movement.

Honey clutched her chest and laughed with relief. "Oh heavens above, girl, you have *got* to clean up in here!"

Della grimaced. "I know, I'm so sorry. I didn't expect visitors. I just don't know what to do, it's all so overwhelming, so I just leave it, in hopes it'll disappear while I'm out."

The women started laughing, bending double and struggling to regain their breath. Each time one of them saw the look on the others' faces, they fell out again. Soon even Della joined them, seeing the absurdity of the situation.

Finally, they all calmed themselves and Abella rested her arm around Della's shoulders, looking kindly into her eyes. "Oh, Della darling, if only it worked that way. Women everywhere would be able to spend their days with their feet up, sipping glasses of sherry and reading Moliére to their hearts' content," she said in her gentle French burr.

Della sighed. That did sound ideal.

"What does *Señor* White say about it?" asked Francisca, looking around in concern.

"Nothing, though I'm sure he's disappointed. But I think he's so happy I'm feeding him now, he'll put up with just about anything from me."

That set the women off again and they all guffawed as they made their way back to the sitting room. "Well, there is nothing for it," said Abella with a frown. "We must help you clean up. We show you how it's done, then you can make this place into a home for your wonderful husband."

"Oh, thank you—I'd love some help." Della felt the tears threatening again and wondered if she had become the kind of woman who cried at everything. A few weeks earlier, she wouldn't have been able to remember the last time she'd wept, but now everything was different. "Do you really think he's wonderful?"

All three women stared at Della in surprise. "What do you mean?" asked Francisca. "You do not know that about *Señor* White yourself?"

"Well…he seems nice, but…"

Honey interrupted with a wave of her hand. "Oh dear, he's just about the kindest man you'll find in this town. Or anywhere else, really."

Abella nodded. "*Oui, vraiment bien, bien. Monsieur* White never visits the dance halls or the saloons, I know this for certain. He does not drink away his wages. He works hard and runs a fair business. My darling husband always says he would work with Clement White any day of the week, because he treats his customers with respect and is honorable in his dealings."

Della's mouth fell open and she arched an eyebrow. "Really?"

"Yes!" all three women said at once, their eyes fixed on hers.

Her heart warmed at their words. She knew her husband was a good man from how he'd treated her since she'd arrived. She just hadn't realized quite how blessed she was to have found him. Truly, she probably didn't deserve such a man, given the history of her own character—she'd begun to realize over the weeks she'd spent in Livingston that she'd previously lived a selfish, vapid existence. It seemed her husband had done just the opposite.

When Clem walked wearily up the staircase toward his apartment that evening, a pleasant aroma drifted down to greet him and he smiled in anticipation of the meal that lay ahead. Ever since Honey Barnes had started teaching Della how to cook, he'd seen a new talent arise in his young wife. She took great pleasure in trying out dishes, and each time he sighed in appreciation or sang her praises, she glowed a little brighter and smiled a little wider. She was changing right before his eyes. He had to admit, it was more than he'd believed possible, or even hoped for, when she'd first arrived.

The only thing he worried about—and it wasn't so much a complaint as it was concern for their health— was the state of the apartment. She lived like a slob— every piece of clothing she took off, she simply discarded where she stood. Every dish, plate or cup she used she stacked on the kitchen table. He didn't know how much longer he could put up with it. He'd been a fastidious man when he'd lived alone. But a little voice inside his head told him to wait a little longer, that if he jumped in to rescue her every time something was difficult, she'd never learn to embrace her new life. And what would become of them if God blessed them with children? He wouldn't have time to run the bank and do all the housework, especially once they moved to the ranch house he'd dreamed of for so many years.

When he reached the door, he was floored. The entire apartment was lit by a series of lanterns set jauntily around the place. There were no dirty clothes on the settee or armchair. A bunch of fresh wildflowers stood in a vase in the center of a clean coffee table. He removed his hat and hung it on the coat rack beside Della's bonnet. "Della?" he called.

There was a rustle from the bedroom and Della emerged, pretty as a prairie hen, an apron tied neatly around her small waist. She smiled and hurried to embrace him, much to his surprise. "Clem, you're home. Did you have a nice day?"

"Yes, I did, thank ya. Though I'm glad to be home."

She smiled. "Well, go wash up for supper. We're having chicken and dumplings tonight, with carrots and fresh-baked bread."

As he washed up, he wondered what was going on. He glanced around the bedroom, looking for the mounds of soiled clothing undoubtedly stashed somewhere. But the room sparkled like a new pin—the bed was made, the floor cleared of all debris. Even the furniture shone as though it had been polished.

He marched back into the kitchen to help Della with the meal, but she'd already set everything on the dining table and stood waiting for him by his chair. The table was clean, another vase of freshly cut flowers, and all the dishes washed and stacked neatly on their shelves. "What's happened in here?" he stammered.

"I cleaned up," Della announced with glee. "Well, not alone. Honey, Francisca and Abella came over and showed me how to wash dishes, scrub dirty laundry, make beds, dust, even polish furniture. What do you think?"

He nodded in silence, spinning around to take it all in. "It's amazin', Della. Yer amazin'." He saw her eyes fill with satisfaction at his words. With a few short strides, he was by her side and wrapped his arms around her, making her gasp. "Darlin', I'm so proud of ya. Ya tackle every obstacle ya meet and ya do it with so much grace. I couldn't ask for a more wonderful wife."

Her eyes filled with tears, one escaping to run down her pink cheek. He wiped it away with a fingertip, then kissed the cheek where the tear had carved its path. His lips traveled downward, kissing gently and tenderly as he went, until he reached her parted lips. She trembled in his arms, and he could bear it no longer.

She'd awakened feelings in him he never thought possible. She was so beautiful, and right before his eyes she was transforming from a self-centered, spoiled city girl into a woman of substance. In the past few weeks, she'd shown kindness to him, and to others—he'd heard how she'd helped Honey, who'd come to the bank the previous day, asking about a loan. She wanted to start a business, selling homemade meals to the working-men of the town, thanks to Della's idea and encouragement. He'd never have believed the woman he met at the train station could become the amazing woman who shivered so enticingly in his arms.

With a soft groan, he pulled her tighter and pressed his lips against hers. She melted in his embrace, and her lips sought his hungrily, exciting a new level of desire within him.

When he pulled away, her eyes were still closed, her lashes dark half moons against her pale cheeks. He smiled and kissed her forehead softly. "Shall we eat, Mrs. White?" he asked with a smirk.

Her eyes fluttered open and she sighed. "Yes. Let's eat."

They sat at the table, and this time when he said the blessing, she finally seemed comfortable holding his hand. The meal tasted as delicious as it smelled. He felt as if he'd fallen into some kind of dream where everything he'd ever hoped for was coming true. He smiled at the thought. "How're ya doin', Della? Ya finally growin' to like it here in Livingston?"

She paused for a moment, her spoon poised over her bowl. "I suppose it's growing on me. Though I do miss my family—my cousin Effie especially. She was my best friend in the whole wide world, and now she's somewhere in Oregon. I miss my sisters and all my other friends. I miss the balls and soirees and wagon rides through Central Park and going to shows on Broadway. Livingston is…"

"What?" he gently urged.

"It's…ugly," she said, her cheeks blushing pink. "I'm sorry, I know I sound ungrateful. But this town is so raw and dusty and full of dirty, smelly, unkempt miners."

He laughed. "That's true. Though the territory's as beautiful as any landscape ya can find, I'd reckon."

She nodded. "I do enjoy looking at the mountains in the distance. They are pretty."

He laid down his spoon and took her hand. "I'll tell ya what, darlin'. How about we go outta town in the wagon after church tomorrow? We'll have a picnic, 'n I can take ya to see someplace that's special for me. What do ya say?"

She nodded and dipped her spoon into the soup, finding a dumpling. "That sounds nice," she said.

He grinned. "Yer gonna love it."

Chapter Seven

The church pew was hard, and Della fidgeted, smoothing her skirts over her bent knees and tucking her crossed ankles demurely below her seat. She smiled at Clem who sat beside her, then stood, one gloved hand on his strong forearm, as they sang the final hymn.

As soon as the service was over, Honey rushed to her side, her grin wide. She kissed Della's cheek and took her hands between her own. "Della, how are you?"

"Fine, thank you. How about you?"

"Fine, fine. You know, I completely sold out yesterday—can you believe it? I'm baking all day while the kids are at school and it's all selling! Yesterday's pies were all that was left over from Friday's baking and now they're gone as well. It's wonderful! Thank you so much for the idea and for buying the ingredients to get me started." She held her breath a moment and glanced at Clem. "Sorry," she mouthed to Della.

Clem stared straight ahead, pretending he didn't hear, but a hint of a smile snuck across his mouth.

Della shook her head with a laugh. "It's fine."

Just then, Francisca and Abella joined them. Francisca wore an impressive hat with a cockade of black and blue feathers to match her black gown. Ringlets cascaded down from a high pile of curls on top of her head. Abella's style was more severe, with a tight bun and a fitted gray gown with white lace trim. "I have had a wonderful idea," said Francisca with a laugh. "We should all go mining next Saturday."

"Mining?" Della frowned and crossed her arms over her chest. "I'm not sure I like the sound of that."

"It is not mining, really," said Abella, playfully slapping Francisca's arm. "Panning for gold. You stand in a creek bed and swirl water and silt around in a pan. Any gold you find, you keep. What could be better?"

"Do tell," added Honey, one eyebrow arched.

"Well, you know Hans pans for gold," Francisca explained. "He used to do more, but now he works at the lumber yard most days. Still, he goes when he can—he says it is soothing, and he finds a nugget sometimes. He asks and asks me to go with him, and I have not—it sounded so dull. But if I have friends with me, it might be fun. We could pack a picnic lunch and take a walk. What do you think?"

Della looked at Clem, who smiled back. "That sounds nice," he said. "We'd love to come—wouldn't we, Della?"

Della clapped her hands and grinned. "Oh yes, we would."

"That's it then—I'm in," said Honey with a snap of her fingers. "Well, if I can bring the kids…"

"Of course," Francisca assured her. "They will be no trouble."

Abella nodded. "I am sure Stanley would enjoy it too. We will be there."

* * *

The clip-clop of the horses' hooves on the trails set a steady rhythm and Della found herself humming along to it. She blushed when she realized what she was doing and smiled.

"Don't stop," said Clem with a grin. "Ya got a lovely voice. I could listen to it all day long."

She laughed. "You're too kind."

"So," he said, "what do ya think of the view now? Not so ugly anymore?"

She shook her head. "Not ugly at all—it's spectacular. You were right—we just needed to get out of town. It can be a bit much, all the drunken shouting and bawdy laughter, the dance hall pianos and fiddles and the constant drone of the flies. And the dust—ugh!"

His eyebrows shot skyward and he chuckled beneath his breath. "It ain't that bad, is it?"

"I suppose not. But it is nice to be out in the country."

"I reckon New York City gets purty ugly at times too." He pushed his hat back with one hand and shifted the reins into the other.

"Yes, it can. But where we lived on the Upper East Side was lovely. The streets were swept clean, and the lawns were covered in brilliant green grass, all manicured to perfection. The houses were well-maintained and painted in soft colors. And there were plenty of trees in our neighborhood. I loved the trees—in the fall, their trunks would be black and stark against the oranges, reds and yellows of the leaves before they drifted to the ground. Oh, it was lovely. Of course, plenty of places in the city weren't as pretty, but our street was beautiful." Her mind drifted, pondering happy childhood memories.

He slipped an arm behind her back and pulled her close. "It'll be beautiful here too one day, mark my words," he whispered against her hair before kissing it softly.

She laid her head on his shoulder, sighed and listened to the birds trilling around them.

The trail led down to a bubbling brook, and Clem pulled up on the reins. He helped Della from the wagon, his hands wrapped firmly about her waist, and set her on the ground. "Does this suit?" he asked, motioning toward the creek bed.

"It's perfect," sighed Della. She lifted a hand to shield her eyes from the sun's glare and spotted a large oak tree by the water's edge. Its sprawling branches shaded the creek bank, and its strong trunk looked like the perfect place to rest one's back.

Clem fixed the horse a feed bag, then handed Della a picnic rug. Hoisting the basket of food out of the wagon bed, he offered her his arm and they walked together toward the oak. Della spread the blanket out in the shade and sat down, tucking her feet beneath her. Clem settled beside her and passed her the basket.

"Let's see now," she began, opening the basket. "There's fried chicken, potatoes, bread rolls and apple pie." She pulled each item out as she spoke and laid them on the blanket.

Clem plucked a daisy from the ground beside him and leaned forward to tuck it behind Della's ear. His hand strayed from the flower and ran down the side of her face and the length of her neck. "Beautiful, just like you," he said shyly.

"Thank you." Her cheeks flushed with warmth and she felt a bubble of happiness well up within her.

He sat back and slipped his hat from his head, setting it on the blanket beside him. "Ya know, I never imagined I'd be so blessed to find a wife as beautiful, smart and fun as ya are."

"Well, you're not quite what I expected either," she said with a smirk.

He burst out in a loud guffaw and she joined him. "I'll bet," he said once he caught his breath. Then, more seriously, "But I hope it ain't all bad."

She patted his arm gently. "No, not all bad. Not bad at all."

He tore his eyes from hers and pointed across the stream. "Over yonder on the other side of the brook is my land."

Della frowned and sat up straighter, peering in the direction he pointed. "What? What do you mean, your land?"

"It's my homestead. It was granted to me by the government—I own it."

She frowned. "You own that land over there?"

"Yep. A hundred and sixty acres worth."

Della gaped. That was a quarter-mile of land—a plot that size in New York City would make a man a millionaire! "Wh-what do you intend to do with it?"

He slid onto his side and rested his head on his hand. "Most of it I'll divvy up and sell. But I plan to keep a few acres and make it into a little ranch someday. Whaddaya think of that?" he asked with a grin.

"I'm not entirely sure. Don't you like being a banker?"

He chuckled. "Yes, I do, and I don't intend to give

it up. But I'd also like to raise a few horses—I've always loved horses, Morgans especially. Ma and Pa had
a horse ranch, 'n I used to train the horses and ride 'em
everywhere. Beautiful creatures." He stuck a piece of
grass between his teeth and began to chew it slowly,
scanning the sky overhead with narrowed eyes. "They
lost their ranch to the bank after the war. I decided
then that one day I'd own a Morgan ranch. And in the
meantime, I'd start my own bank so no one could ever
take the ranch from me."

"Oh, I see." Della's chest tightened at his words. It
was obvious he'd been through pain just as she had.
He understood how it felt to lose everything, since he'd
once been in a similar situation. She drew in a deep
breath and smiled. "Well, I think it will make a beautiful horse ranch. It's just about perfect."

"Ya think ya'd mind livin' all the way out here?" he
asked, concerned.

"It's not so far. Besides, no saloons, no dance halls,
no drunken miners brawling or singing—I'm sure I'd
absolutely love it." They both laughed again as Della
fixed Clem a plate of food.

He took it hungrily, his fingers caressing hers as he
did. "Thank you."

"You're welcome." Della watched him take a bite
of the fried chicken and relished his enjoyment of the
dish. The confession of his hopes and dreams for the
future had surprised her—she'd never considered that
he might wish for more than what he had now. She'd
resigned herself to spend their lives living above the
bank in that cramped apartment, even pictured it teem-
ing with children fighting over who got to sleep against
the wall and who had to share the sofa.

Yet this…she smiled to herself. She could definitely imagine living out here in a comfortable ranch house, with horses grazing nearby and majestic mountain peaks framing the northern horizon. That was a future she could look forward to.

Chapter Eight

Francisca slid down the creek bank with a screech and landed on her rear in the mud, then threw her hands in the air and laughed out loud. Honey and her five children soon followed, each one careening down in the same fashion. Squeals filled the air, along with laughter and the chatter of easy conversation.

Della smiled. She was about to pan for gold for the first time, and she shivered with excitement—what if she found a gold nugget? There was certainly a chance, though Hans Schmidt had said the area had been mostly stripped clean during the gold rush of the 1860s. Still, she found herself flush with nerves that it was even possible. She walked behind Abella as the rest of the group worked their way down toward the rushing waters below. She could feel Clem behind her, the tingle in her back when his fingertips brushed against her. They didn't often get an entire day to spend together and she'd been looking forward to this outing all week.

Once they reached the creek bed, Hans handed out pans and showed them how to fill them with sand and water from the stream, then tip the pan back and forth, back and forth, checking all the while for any flashes within. A long timber flume left over from the '60s ran along one side of the creek, the sluice at the end sitting just above the water's surface. The worn structure had broken in places and was bleached a dull gray by the sun. Della studied it with interest, running her hand along the edge of it. "Ouch!"

"What's wrong?" asked Clem. He carried his full pan to where she stood, sloshing water as he walked.

"Nothing really. I just got a splinter in my finger."

He reached for her hand. "Want me to take a look?"

She pulled it away with a gasp. "No!"

He lifted his palm toward her and chuckled. "Never mind."

She sighed and ducked her head. "I'm sorry, I'm not very good with splinters. Father used to force me to sit while he plucked them out with a needle."

He grimaced. "Well, I promise not to do that—'less you ask me to, of course."

"Which I won't," she quickly added.

He winked at her. "Come on, then—let's go panning." Her face warmed as he curled an arm around her shoulders and they wandered to the water's edge.

They squatted beside the rushing water, dug their pans into the sand and dirt, then lifted them to rock back and forth, letting the water gradually drain over the edges. "Hmmm…no gold here," said Clem with a feigned sigh. "Guess I'll just hafta keep my bank."

Della laughed and dug up another measure of sand. "I suppose so. And I'll just have to, um…" She paused. What *did* she do? It seemed strange to think of it. In New York she'd helped her mother raise funds for various causes, she had a busy social calendar, was in-

volved in church events and even helped families of
war veterans. Since arriving here she'd learned to cook
and clean, while waiting for her head to stop spinning
from all she'd been through. She realized she'd even-
tually have to come up with something to occupy her
time in Livingston.

Clem had noticed her hesitation. "Well, ya can keep
helpin' Honey grow her business. 'Fore you know it,
she'll be runnin' the whole town."

"I suppose—but the business is hers, not mine. I
hadn't thought about it much until now, but I don't
seem to have found anything yet in Livingston that's
just…mine." She sighed and pushed the pan back into
the water.

Clem shifted his hat back with his fingertips and
caught her eye. "Yeah, but ya ain't been here that long. I
know it might seem like a long while, but ya got plenty
of time, a lifetime, to figure it all out."

"I suppose you're right." She nodded and swished
the pan back and forth. Her haunches were beginning
to tire—she'd have to stand up soon or she'd cramp.

"What would ya like to do? I always figgered we'd
start a family…ya know, when yer ready. And that'll
sure keep ya busy." He chuckled.

She smiled wryly, tipping her head to one side and
meeting his gaze. "I do want to have a family one day.
But I want more than that. I want to do something…
meaningful."

He grinned and winked. "Well, I got a few ideas…"

She knew just what he was insinuating, the mis-
chievous cad. Her cheeks colored and she slapped him
playfully on the arm.

He pretended to wince. "Ow! Yer stronger than ya look," he teased.

She glanced down at her pan, "Oh, Clem, look! Gold!"

He stood and leaned over her shoulder to peer into her pan as well. "Well, how 'bout that—sure looks like it all right. That's what ya can do with yer life— be a gold miner. It's meaningful, it's fulfillin' and it'll make us rich!" He let his pan drop on the creek bank and held his sides while he laughed.

She stood and set her pan carefully beside his, then reached into the creek, lifted some water in her hands and threw it at him. His eyes widened in surprise as the cold liquid soaked through his shirt, then leaped for her with a shout of glee. She turned and ran, sloshing along the water's edge, her boots and stockings soon soaked completely through. The others stopped panning to watch, laugh and shout encouragement.

It didn't take him long to catch her and grab her around the waist, and she gasped and squealed as she lost her foothold and they both fell into the creek. She went under and tried to get her feet beneath her, but her boots could get no purchase on the smooth rocks lining the creek bed. He lifted her and set her right, and she found that the water only came up to her chest. She took a deep breath in relief, filling her hungry lungs with air.

Clem stood in front of her, his arms still around her waist. He shook the water from his hair and his eyes sparkled as he grinned at her.

She frowned and pushed against him with both hands. She'd have stomped her foot too, if it hadn't been in three feet of freezing water. "Clement White, you scoundrel—you did that on purpose! Now I'm soaked to the bone."

He tipped back his head and guffawed. He was enjoying every moment of this, and that only made her madder. "This is not funny!" She enunciated each word to emphasize just how upset with him she was. But it only made him laugh harder.

Then he pulled her close, their wet clothes smacking against each other. He lowered his head and kissed her passionately on the lips. Her eyes drifted closed, and she snuck her hands up around his neck and laced her fingers into his hair. His lips sought hers hungrily, wanting more, and she trembled from head to toe like ripples through the creek water.

Suddenly, she became keenly aware of eyes on them. She pulled away and covered her mouth with her hand. "Er, Clem…"

"Don't stop on our account," said Honey with a laugh. "You two are just about the cutest thing I've seen in a while."

Della felt her entire body flush with warmth, and she backed away from Clem with a smile. His eyes were still on hers—he hadn't flinched away like she had. She could see his desire there, running deep and strong like the water surrounding them. She squeezed the damp from her hair as best she could, then waded back to shore. One thing was certain—Clem was not the dull, straight-laced banker she'd first believed him to be. Not by a long shot.

The wagon ride home from the panning outing to the gold fields was jovial and full of good-humored teasing from everyone about their little romp in the creek. Clem laughed along with the rest. He'd been worried for a few moments that Della might stay mad at him about being dunked like that, but the kiss seemed to soften her up pretty well. He grinned at the memory of his lips on hers and the way her wet hair clung to her face. She leaned against him now, her arm looped through his, her head on his shoulder. He liked the feeling.

He'd finally begun to believe that sending away for a bride wasn't such a bad idea after all. In fact, it might turn out to be the best idea he ever had at this rate. He lifted a hand to caress her now-dry hair and felt his heart soar. He'd hoped to find someone to share his life with, perhaps have a family with. He never imagined she'd make him so happy. But happy he was, almost giddy. Now he was anxious to get her home—he'd arranged a surprise for her with the help of their friends and her Bible study group. He couldn't wait to see the look on her face.

Della sighed and lifted her head from Clem's shoulder reluctantly. They were home after the most delightful day, with the most delightful friends—and the most delightful kiss. She didn't even mind that the gold she'd discovered had turned out to be worthless pyrite—"fool's gold," Hans had called it.

Clem climbed from the wagon and offered her his hand, and she stepped down behind him. Her dress had dried on the long ride home, and even though she knew she likely looked a fright, at least she was no longer dripping. They waved goodbye to the rest of the group and climbed the stairs wearily to their apartment. She was looking forward to bathing, changing and settling on the love seat to read a book. An evening at home with her husband was just what she needed after the long day. The thought surprised her—back home, she'd always been eager to find the next gathering, party or lavish affair. She grinned at the realization of how much she'd changed since moving to Livingston.

The apartment was warm and cozy when they arrived, though dark. It was almost sunset and the rooms lay in shadow. She hurried to light a couple of lanterns, then carried one to the bedroom to freshen up.

A gentle knock at the door startled her, and she quickly pulled her bodice back up where she'd unbuttoned it. "Yes?"

Clem poked his head in and grinned. "I got a surprise for ya."

"What kind of surprise?"

"Well, ya'll just hafta wait and see. But how 'bout ya slip into one of yer party dresses for me and fix ya hair? 'Cause I'm takin' ya out."

She gasped. "Truly?"

"Yes indeed, Mrs. White." He ducked out, pulling the door closed.

Della regarded her reflection in the looking glass. They were going out! Other than her weekly Bible study, she hadn't been out at night since arriving in town. She'd assumed Clem was a confirmed homebody, but it seemed he was making her question all her assumptions about him today. But what could they do in Livingston on a Saturday night? She certainly didn't want to join the rowdies at the saloons or the crowds at the dance halls.

She washed up quickly and chose a cornflower blue dress with a demure neckline and a shawl to match. She brushed out her long dark hair in slow, even strokes until it shone, then fixed it up in great loops on either side of her face and pinned the rest into a bun at the back of her head. A necklace and earrings completed the ensemble. Satisfied, she grabbed her reticule and hurried out to the kitchen. Clem, already washed and dressed in a black frock coat and striped trousers, took her arm and they were on their way. A wagon was waiting for them downstairs; a stable boy held the horse's reins with a shy smile. Clem handed him a coin and he ran, no doubt back home to where his mother awaited him with a warm supper.

Clem climbed into the wagon beside her and slapped the reins on the horse's back. They rode down the street and through the center of town beneath a canopy of sparkling stars, past the drunks already falling out of doorways and the saloon girls leaning out their windows calling to passersby.

Before long, the white steeple of the little church rose against the dark horizon and Della spied a string of twinkling lights lining the pasture beside it. She turned to Clem with a quizzical look. "What's that?"

He laughed, but didn't say a word.

Now she saw the lines of wagons and hobbled horses grazing nearby. And there was a band—fiddles, harmonicas and even a piano accordion. She clapped her hands and her eyes shone. "Is it a dance, Clem?"

"Yep, sure is. I just figgered ya'd gone without so much. At least I could put on a dance for ya."

She flung her arms around his neck with a shout and kissed him resoundingly on the cheek.

The wagon stopped beside the others, and she could barely wait for him to help her down. She could already see Honey, Abella and Francisca waiting for her with grins on their faces. The rest of the Bible study group was there too, along with most of the church congregation from what she could tell. She waved to them all and waited while Clem hobbled the horse. Then with her arm nestled in his, they strode over to greet everyone. The band began to play and couples lined a dance floor freshly cut into the churchyard grass. Others sat around on picnic rugs, eating finger foods, drinking punch and conversing. Lanterns hung from trees all around them, making it a twinkling wonderland. Della held her breath as she took it all in. It was marvelous.

"I told you, *ma chere*, he is a good man," Abella whispered in her ear before swinging away on her husband's arm to join the others on the dance floor.

"You did all this for me?" she whispered, her eyes filling with tears.

"Sure did. Would ya care to dance?" Clem bowed gallantly before her with a sparkle in his eye.

"Why, yes, I would—thank you, kind sir." She offered an exaggerated curtsy of her own.

He laughed and pulled her into his arms, pressing her hard against his wide chest. He smiled and kissed her first on the nose, then softly on the lips, before pulling her behind him. She laughed and before long they were two-stepping to the beat of the music as it soared over the dusty little town. For this one evening, everything was perfect.

When they returned home late that night, Della felt as though she could barely stand a moment longer. Her feet ached, her legs throbbed and her head spun. Music still resounded in her ears and she hummed along to it, making Clem glance at her every now and then with a smile.

She climbed the stairs on her own while he settled the horse in the stable. After washing up for bed, she crawled into a nightgown and brushed her hair again so it hung long and shining down her back. She yawned wide and lifted her arms over her head in satisfaction.

The bedroom door swung open and Clem staggered in, wheezing from the climb up the staircase. "Did you run up the stairs?" asked Della with a chuckle.

"Um…yep. I did."

"Why…?"

He reached her in three long strides and lifted her into his arms, cradling her like a child. She gasped in surprise, but couldn't speak a word when she saw the look in his eyes. He laid her gently on the bed, then kissed her long and slow, his lips devouring hers.

"Clem?" she asked, her throat tight.

"Yes, my darling?"

"Thank you for tonight, it was wonderful."

He smiled. "You're welcome my love. And it's not over yet."

Her eyes widened, and she leaned up to kiss him again.

Chapter Nine

Della stood in the middle of the post office and held the letter between trembling hands. It was from Father in New York, and she hadn't the nerve to open it yet. What if it was further bad news? She didn't think she could take hearing anything worse from home, especially when she was so far away and could do nothing to help.

Instead, she tucked it into her reticule and headed for the bank. She'd agreed to let Clem show her around today. He was so excited to show off his business to her, even offering to train her how to be a teller. She'd suggested that he might need her if one of the other tellers decided to leave or was out sick. She liked the idea of counting money and chatting with customers. It could be fun. His only concern was that he was hoping they'd have a baby before too long.

That thought made her nerves flutter like a pack of butterflies. It wasn't that she didn't want a family, but sometimes she still felt like a child herself, and didn't know the first thing about raising a baby. It was the kind of thing a woman needed her mother close by to help with, but she knew that wasn't possible, and the thought made her throat tighten.

And now there was a letter from home, a letter she couldn't bring herself to read.

She pushed through the bank's front door and waved to Tobias the guard. He nodded and smiled, tugging the bill of his cap. She walked to Clem's office, rapped on the door, then opened it with a half-smile. "Well, here I am, boss—ready to learn."

He stood to wrap his arms around her, kissed her hard on the mouth and ran a hand up her back, twisting his fingers into her loose hair.

"Now, now, *Mr. White*," she chastised him, extricating herself. "This is really not the time nor the place."

He groaned and rolled his eyes, running his fingers through his hair. "All business today, huh? Well, let's get started then."

A few hours later, after Clem had shown her how everything worked, she walked out of the bank, stopping to chat with customers as she went, and headed across the street to check on Honey and Abella. Honey's business had expanded so rapidly she'd rented a space across the street and hired Abella as her assistant. "Honey's" was now an honest-to-goodness restaurant, and Della smiled up at the large sign hanging above the door. She pushed it open, setting a bell ringing above her head.

Honey glanced up from where she stood in the kitchen, her hair in a net, a clean white apron wrapped around her shapely waist. "Good day to you, Della!"

Della waved, took a seat at the counter, and Abella set a cup of coffee in front of her with a smile. "You want lunch, *oui*?" she asked, one hand on her thin hip.

"Yes, please," said Della, taking a sip of the steaming black liquid. "Lunch for two, to take home with me."

"Oh, so romantic! I am sure we can do that. What will you have?"

"Can we please have chicken pot pie, mashed potatoes with gravy and…for dessert I think we'll have molasses stack cake."

Abella pursed her lips. "Ooh, good choices. Coming right away…no, no—*up*. Right *up*." She delivered the order to Honey, came back and leaned her elbows on the counter, resting her chin in her hands. "So, how are things with *Monsieur* Clem?"

Della blushed and lowered her gaze to the coffee cup. "Things are…wonderful."

"Ooh, wonderful is good," mooned Abella, a dreamy look in her eyes. "You treat that man well—he is one of the best."

Della nodded just as Honey brought out her order wrapped in brown paper. "I don't usually let people take my good pie pans home with them, but for you I'll make an exception. Now be careful, it's hot." She winked at Della and patted her arm.

"I'll bring the dishes back as soon as I can," said Della, taking the package from Honey with a smile. "Thank you—it smells divine."

"Well, you're welcome. Are you coming to Bible study tonight?"

"I certainly am—I'll see you there," called Della over her shoulder as she waltzed back out through the door, setting off the bell once again.

She went up to the apartment, laid the food on the kitchen table and shook the kinks out of her arms. Her eyes fell on the envelope beside the stack of food, and she knew she couldn't keep putting it off. Even if the news was bad, she had to know. She missed her family, and the letter might contain details about her sisters and cousins, where they were, how they were doing…

With a sigh, she quickly tore it open and read the words scrawled in her father's familiar hand.

My dearest Della,

I write to inform you that the scoundrel who ruined our family's livelihood and reputation has been found out! He is being brought to justice and has admitted to the lies he told. I am in the process of restoring to our family everything we lost, along with our good name. You will be happy to know that I expect to rebuild my business, purchase a new home and retrieve the life we lost.

I know this news may come too late for you, and I am sorry about that. Your sisters are well and settled with their new husbands. I have enclosed details of their whereabouts.

Your mother is well, also. She took ill after you all left and has spent a good deal of time in bed, though seems better now. She is happy about this news, but misses you all terribly, as do I. The boys miss you too, in their own way. Tommy turned fifteen last week, and Danny will be thirteen soon. They each work a paper route, but otherwise seem not to have been very much upset by the scandal.

I hope this correspondence finds you well.

Please reply and tell us how you fare. Let us know if you are able to return home; we will send funds to cover your travel expenses.

Your ever loving father,
Septimus Stout

Della gasped and the letter fluttered to the floor. Everything would be worked out! Father was restoring their lost fortune and all was well. This was much better news than she could have hoped for. But...what did it mean for her?

With a heavy heart, she glanced around the small apartment, taking in the chipped paint, simple furnishings and cheery fresh flowers. She'd embraced this place as her home, believing she would never return to New York. And now she was married. What should she do? What *could* she do? She couldn't leave Clem, not now. She loved him, and knew without a doubt he loved her. Yet would she willingly stay here, knowing she could return to the life she once had if she chose to?

A noise on the staircase startled her and she forced a smile onto her face. There was no need to worry Clem with the news just yet. She'd have to think about it and make a decision before she brought it to him. She wanted to stay with him—she was happy here—but could she bear never seeing her family again? She wasn't sure she could face that now, knowing they wanted her home. Would Clem consider moving to New York? She hurried to set the table, then greeted Clem as he appeared at the top of the stairs.

He grinned and stepped close to give her a kiss,

wrapping her warmly in his arms. "Hello, darlin' wife. What have we here?" He eyed the food she'd laid out.

"Lunch," she said with a grin. She slipped from his embrace and finished readying the meal. "Honey made it, so it's bound to be delicious."

"Oh? What's the special occasion?" He removed his hat and hurried to wash up.

"Nothing special, really. I just wanted to give you a treat."

"Well, ya sure have," he called from the bedroom, soon emerging with a clean face and wiping his hands on a towel. He set the towel on the table and took his seat. "This looks wonderful—thank ya."

Della sat beside him and took his hand as he blessed the food, then took a bite of the pot pie, still steaming hot. "Mmmm…"

Clem licked his lips. "No wonder she's doin' so well over there—this is delicious."

Della smiled. "How is your day going so far?"

"Purty well. Mr. Handley wants to expand the lumber yard, so I'm gonna help him with a loan. It's a solid business, and his plan makes sense. He's a good man and always pays on time. I think it'll be a fine partnership." He took another bite of pie.

"That sounds good." Della's mind was still on the letter—she couldn't stop thinking about what might be happening that very moment back home. Had they found a house? What about all their things—were they able to recover them?

"Have you heard from your folks back in New York yet?" asked Clem, one eyebrow raised.

She coughed, almost spraying pie. Plucking her napkin from her lap, she quickly covered her mouth and dabbed around the edges. "Excuse me, I'm sorry. Uh… no, not yet." She didn't want to be dishonest with him, but she was panicked. She just needed to buy herself a little time so she could think it over.

He lay his fork down on the table and took her hand. With a kiss on her fingers, he enveloped her hand in his and met her gaze, his warm brown eyes full of love and concern. "I was thinkin'…how 'bout we save for a li'l trip back east on the train next year? We could go and visit yer folks, maybe buy ya a few dresses and such. What do ya think of that?"

Her eyes went wide and she squealed. "Truly, Clem? You'd do that?"

"Sure, why not? If that's what ya want."

"But it's so expensive." She frowned and pursed her lips.

"Yes, but we can make do without somethin' else if visiting yer family means that much to ya." He brought her hand up to his lips and kissed it again.

She leaped to her feet and slipped onto his lap, wrapping her arms around his neck and kissing him hard on the mouth. "Clem, you are too good to me."

"Well, I dunno 'bout that," he said, his cheeks reddening. "I'd say we're good to each other." He stood to his feet, his strong arms easily lifting her, and carried her toward the bedroom, kicking the door shut behind them.

Della sighed, letting her eyes drift closed as he carried her—lunch could wait.

Epilogue

Della fixed her small straw hat with its single dashing feather. She pushed it back and to the left a little, but it kept falling to one side. She'd have to redo it at lunch time. For now, she was filling as teller—Francisca had taken the morning off.

She grinned as the front door opened and Honey Barnes marched in with a stack of paperwork. She wore a simple but professional dress with buttons up the front of the bodice, a high neckline and puffed sleeves. Her expression was serious and she strode over to Della's window. "Good morning—I've come to speak with Clem. Is he in?"

"Why, Honey—you're very formal today. Yes, he's in his office. Come on through and I'll take you to him." Della stood and ran her hands over her swollen belly. She smiled down at the growing bump as she hurried to let Honey in through the gate.

They met Clem in his office and he waved them inside with a grin. "Ladies, please take a seat. How can I help ya?"

Honey sat across from him and laid the papers on

top of his desk. "Mr. White—Clem—as you know, 'Honey's' has become quite a successful business in a very short amount of time."

He nodded. "Indeed it has. Ya worked hard and did a fine job."

She smiled nervously. "Thank you. Anyway, we need to expand, and I have to buy supplies and hire more staff and pay rent and so on. I don't have the cash for a big expansion, so I'm here to show you my accounts and ask for another loan. I know I'm not quite through paying off the last one yet, but I do need your help."

Clem leaned forward, took the paperwork and flipped through it slowly, studying the numbers and occasionally making tallies on a scrap of paper. Honey glanced at Della with a furrowed brow, and Della gave her an encouraging smile.

Finally he sat back with a smile and linked his hands behind his head. "Well, Mrs. Barnes, your accounts are in fine shape. I agree that you should expand and I can see that you'll be profitable enough to make the required repayments, in addition to the ones you're already making. I'll give you the loan."

Honey jumped to her feet, took his hand and shook it vigorously. "Thank you, Clem, thank you. I'm so very grateful to you—both of you." She hugged Della and the two women laughed together as they left Clem's office.

"You're getting to be quite the tycoon," said Della with a chuckle.

Honey grimaced. "That sounds frightful. But when I think about cooking for people, it sounds just about perfect. I love it—I think that's why it's going so well."

"I think so too."

"How are you feeling?" asked Honey, eyeing Della's round stomach.

"Better now. The first few months were hard, but I'm all right these days."

"When do you and Clem leave for New York?"

"Soon after the baby comes. I'm so looking forward to it—I can't wait!" She kissed Honey on the cheek and said goodbye, then returned to Clem's office where he was bent over a file on his desk. She pushed the door closed, sashayed over and sat on his knee.

"Ooof!" he said with a mock grimace.

She slapped his shoulder playfully. "Don't you dare complain about how heavy I am. It's all your fault."

He grinned. "Now, I know yer over the moon about it. 'N so am I." He placed a hand on her stomach and rubbed it gently, then cupped her face in his hands and kissed her gently.

She grinned, remembering the way his handsome face had paled when she'd told him about the letter from her father, asking her to return home. He'd looked sick over the revelation. But she'd known she couldn't leave him, not when he held her heart the way he did.

"I heard from Father again," she began, running her hand across his firm chest.

"Hmmm?"

"Yes, he says they've found the perfect house, in the same street we used to live on."

He smiled, and cocked his head to one side. "Are you still glad you chose to stay here, with me?"

She kissed him softly. "I am. I know it took me a while, but I fell in love. With you, and this crazy town."

He chuckled, and kissed the tip of her nose, then her lips.

She sighed against his mouth. "Clem, what did I do to deserve you?" she whispered.

"Whatever it was, ya must have been very bad." He winked. "I dunno what I did, 'cause I don't deserve ya at all."

She laid her head on his chest and listened to the steady rhythm of his heart. His arms encircled her shoulders and held her tight against him.

Then, she lifted her eyes to his, and smiled. "Or maybe God just knew we'd be perfect together."

* * * * *

Historical Note & Author's Remarks

When Kit Morgan approached me and asked me to be part of this wonderful series, I jumped at the chance. The concept of debutantes, falling from grace, and becoming mail-order brides was too tempting to pass up. Oh the fun we might have!

You may think that parts of the storyline in *Della* are far-fetched, but as with all of my books, there's a little bit of truth behind every fiction.

When Honey Barnes carves up the saloon bar with an axe, she's following in the path of a young woman who did the same thing many years earlier. Determined to make a statement about the immorality of drinking, carousing and gambling, she took an axe to the place. I thought it was such an interesting incident, I just had to include a similar one in my book!

Livingston was a gold mining town, and it grew up raw and quick in the wild years of Montana Territory's youth. Many women, just like Abella, found themselves in difficult situations and had to turn to prostitution to earn a living. In fact, for a while, there weren't many women in the area other than prostitutes, saloon girls and dancers.

There were also plenty of immigrants from Latin America, just like Francesca. They came up through Panama on steamers, and into California and beyond for the gold rush.

I'm excited about where this series will take us— there are plenty more stories to come, and they'll weave through the generations in a new and fun way, unlike any other series out there.

I hope you enjoyed this little caper through the old west.

Warmest regards,
Vivi Holt

About the Author

Vivi Holt was born in Australia. She grew up in the country, where she spent her youth riding horses at Pony Club, and adventuring through the fields and rivers around the farm. Her father was a builder, turned saddler, and her mother a nurse, who stayed home to raise their four children.

After graduating from a degree in International Relations, Vivi moved to Atlanta, Georgia, to work for a year. It was there that she met her husband, and they were married three years later. She spent seven years living in Atlanta and travelled to various parts of the United States during that time, falling in love with the beauty of that immense country and the American people.

Vivi also studied for a Bachelor of Information Technology, and worked in the field ever since until becoming a full-time writer in 2016. She now lives in Brisbane, Australia, with her husband and three small children. Married to a Baptist pastor, she is very active in her local church.

Follow Vivi Holt
www.viviholt.com
vivi@viviholt.com

HATTIE

Chapter One

The sway of the carriage made Hattie Stout's head loll from side to side. A sudden bump over a particularly large rock whacked her temple against the dull wood window frame. She cried out, rubbing where a lump was beginning to form.

"That was rather an uncomfortable one, wasn't it?" Mrs. Sandringham, the elderly lady seated across from her in the stagecoach, smiled, one hand resting atop her straw hat.

Hattie nodded and pursed her lips. "Rather. How much longer do you think we'll be? I feel as though my brain will be jostled from my head if we don't stop soon." She grimaced and glanced out the window at the green, hilly landscape beyond.

Mrs. Sandringham sighed. "I'm afraid we'll be a couple more hours. They said we should expect to arrive just before sundown. And it's only two o'clock now."

Hattie took a long, slow breath and leaned against

the window frame, her hand protecting her head from further battering. Several more hours...she'd just have to fix her eyes on the horizon to keep the nausea at bay.

She could feel Colin Sandringham's eyes on her as she studiously avoided his gaze. Unlike his mother, he was a sullen, sweaty man. Middle-aged, he'd never married and seemed unable or unwilling to either look away or strike up a conversation with the eighteen-year-old Hattie. She shuddered involuntarily and tugged at the edges of her knit shawl, pulling it tighter around her shoulders.

She'd spent weeks on the road, first chugging along the train tracks westbound from New York City to Sacramento, then doubling back eastward via stagecoach to her final destination: Coloma, described by her father as a small mining town in California. Hattie longed to set her feet on firm ground and keep them there. She'd never traveled so far in her short life and easily became ill from the motion.

But what really made her stomach churn was that she was headed to Coloma to meet her husband-to-be. And given that she'd never even set eyes on the man she was to wed, she couldn't get past the fear that bubbled up whenever she thought of him. Her head grew heavy, pinpricks of light danced before her eyes, and she'd heave in great gasps as though there wasn't enough air left in the world to fill her lungs.

The first time it happened had been directly after Father told her he'd lost the family fortune to a swindler. The second was when Mother broke the news she was to be sent west as a mail-order bride. Now, every time her thoughts drifted to the fate that lay before her, she thought she might die if she weren't able to catch her breath again. Then it would pass, and she'd discover tears on her cheeks and wonder how they'd got there.

She sighed again and traced the outline of the window with the tip of her finger. How she missed home—her sisters, Mother, even Father, though she blamed him for sending her away. She'd pleaded with him—surely there was another way. But he'd turned on his heel and strode from the room, her entreaties bouncing off his sturdy back. Septimus Stout was a hard man—he loved his family, that she knew, but when he made up his mind there was no way she or anyone else could change it. Mother had sobbed quietly at the sideboard as she'd poured herself another snifter of brandy.

She picked at a splinter, tugging it from the windowsill and flicked it out of the coach. Shrubs and trees flashed past the window amidst swirls of dust that curled up from the dirt road. She glanced back, watching the dust billow out behind them like a bridal veil. The thought made her eyes cloud with tears and she dashed them away with the back of her hand.

All her life, she'd dreamt of the wedding she might someday have—hoping, wishing, dreaming that her husband would be a kind, generous and loving man. Handsome as well. But now she was to marry a miner. A miner! The lump that formed in her throat wouldn't budge this time and she swallowed hard around it, determined not to let her tears return.

Only a few short weeks ago, she'd been a debutante—living in New York City in one of the finest houses, on one of the most prestigious streets in that great city. She'd had servants to wait on her and glamorous gowns to fill her closet. Every week she'd attended the most exclusive soirees, balls and events with the rest of the

social elite. She'd been engaged to a handsome gentleman: at least there'd been an understanding between
her and her paramour, even if his family refused to recognize that fact. And now—she was to marry a miner
and live in a small town in California! She didn't know
how she could bear it.

A butterfly landed on the sill, and her eyes widened
in surprise. She watched it crawl along the lip of the
opening, smiled and slipped a finger gently beneath it,
scooping it up so it could walk along the length of it.
She held it close to examine the whorls and circles that
decorated its delicate wings. If she were back home,
she'd have added it to her collection. But the box that
held her treasure of insects, captured over the past ten
years, was three thousand miles away, left behind when
her family moved from her childhood home.

She sighed and held her hand up to the window. The
butterfly leaped into the air and was gone in a moment
as the stage sailed on.

As she stared out into the wilderness beyond, her
gaze caught a thin trail of dust in the distance. It grew
closer by the moment, and before long she saw three
men on horseback rapidly closing in on the stage. The
horses they rode galloped with outstretched necks, and
the men wore hats pulled low over their faces.

With a frown, she leaned further out the window.
The wind caught her hair, almost dislodging her bonnet
and whipping strands of her mahogany locks around
her face. The men drew alongside the stage, and she
realized they had kerchiefs pulled over their mouths
and noses and held pistols aloft as they rode. She fell
back in alarm.

"What is it?" asked Mrs. Sandringham, her eyebrows pulled low over small reddened eyes.

"Outlaws!" exclaimed Hattie, just as the driver of the coach shouted from where he sat high above the horses. She heard him bring down the whip on the horses' backs and the stage sped up, careening along the narrow trail. She was thrown against the coach wall, first on one side, then the other.

She clutched her bonnet and shouted in alarm when Mrs. Sandringham landed on the floor and knocked her forehead on the hard edge of the seat. She helped the woman up again with Colin's aid, but was dismayed to see a line of blood form on the woman's brow. She squeezed Mrs. Sandringham's hand, smiling tightly, even as she used her free hand to steady herself.

A gun shot rang out overhead, and Mrs. Sandringham screamed in fright. Hattie took a quick breath and shut her eyes tight. The horses pulled up short, and Hattie landed heavily in Colin's lap. He blushed and fussed around, helping her back into her seat. Her bonnet hung over her face and her hairpins had fallen out, her hair falling around her cheeks. Hands shaking, she pressed her locks back into place as best she could and tried to steady her breathing, but a thud outside the coach made her cry out. What was going on?

A man appeared at the window, his eyes dark and narrow above a thick nose and greasy brown kerchief. He pulled the door open, clutched Colin's arm and tugged him violently from the coach. Mrs. Sandringham screamed again, then she too was pulled down the single step to the uneven dirt below. The outlaw's face appeared once more and lifted a hand, beckoning for Hattie to come out as well. She stepped down carefully, her eyes wide.

Another of the scoundrels was yanking luggage from the back of the stage. Trunks, carpetbags and satchels fell from the luggage compartment into the dirt, sending clouds of dust into the air and making Hattie cough. She covered her mouth with a gloved hand and squinted into the bright California sun.

The first outlaw handed around an inverted hat. "All right then, everyone gimme yer pocket watches, jewelry, money...put it all here, if ya please."

The Sandringhams quickly removed anything of value they had and lay it in the hat. Hattie frowned—she'd already lost so much, and now she'd lose the pretty necklace Father gave her for her eighteenth birthday and the remaining few coins in her purse. Could things get any worse? She dropped the items into the hat as the lump in her throat grew again.

The man gleefully shoved it all into his pockets, then set the hat back on his head as his compatriot shouted from the back of the coach. He hurried to help, and the two of them hauled luggage toward their horses, laying it on the steeds' backs and tying it down with ropes.

Hattie was glad her trunk was too heavy for the men to carry on horseback. But when she saw her carpetbag being carried away by one of them, she gasped. He wore a tan Stetson and sported a bushy red beard so long that it brushed against his belt. "No! No, please don't take my bag! Please, I need it! You don't understand, you rotten scoundrels! I've left everything and everyone behind in New York to marry a man I've never met in a godforsaken town called Coloma, and everything I have left in the world is in that bag! Please don't take it, I beg you!" She threw herself at the bag, fighting with the man who held it.

He frowned and kicked at her, but the man with the brown kerchief stopped him with a hand on his arm. "Aw, let 'er have it. We got all we need, don't we? She can have this'un."

The man in the tan Stetson glared at his friend, then shoved the bag toward Hattie. The one with the brown kerchief looked at her with deep brown eyes. He had a black beard sprouting around the kerchief, and a jagged scar that wound up his left cheek and past the corner of his left eye.

The three outlaws turned and leaped onto the backs of their horses, whirled them around and disappeared over a rise with a thunder of hooves. Mrs. Sandringham collapsed against the coach with a cry and Colin fussed over her.

Hattie sighed deeply, then turned to see one of the drivers, a young boy called Peter, peer tentatively around the outside of the stage. "They gone, Miss?" he asked, looking around furtively.

She nodded, a hand on her throat. "Yes, they're gone. Where is Mr. Galloway?" She looked for the other driver.

Peter, wide-eyed, shook his head. "They shot him." His gaze fell to the ground and he frowned.

Hattie ran to the front of the wagon and found Mr. Galloway, a middle aged man with a rotund belly, lying dead beside the horses. She covered her mouth with a cry, then turned away as her stomach revolted, leaning against the wheel of the stagecoach.

Peter hurried to her side. "You all right, Miss?"

She nodded and wiped her mouth with her handkerchief. "Yes, thank you, Peter." She straightened and took a quick breath. "Can you drive on your own?"

He dipped his head. "Yes, Miss."

She staggered back to the door of the coach and found Mrs. Sandringham already inside. She climbed in while Colin helped Peter strap Mr. Galloway's body to the back. Glancing back over her shoulder, she saw no sign of the outlaws.

Hattie sank into her seat, her entire body trembling from head to toe, and began to sob.

Sheriff Edward Milton strode down the covered sidewalk. Coloma was a mining town, a leftover from the Gold Rush days, and every part of it was coated in a fine layer of brown dust. He shoved his hands into the pockets of his dungarees, hopped over a steaming pile of horse manure and onto the street.

The stagecoach was due soon, and he always liked to meet it. Generally, Stan Galloway the driver had plenty of news from Folsom and the other stops along the way from Sacramento to Reno. He transported the mailbag as well, and Ed was hoping to hear from his sister back in Virginia. It had been a while since her last correspondence, and she'd been expecting at the time. News of the baby's birth was long overdue—he looked forward to hearing about the seventh addition to their large brood.

He ran a hand over his beard and trotted across the street, weaving between buggies, wagons and cowboys cantering along on the backs of lean stock horses. Most called greetings to him as they passed. Others stared hard ahead pretending not to see him. He didn't take it personally—it went with the territory of being a small-town sheriff. Some people loved him, some hated him. Either way, he always watched his back.

As if on cue, the stage rounded the bend at the end of the street on its way into town. Dust swirled in a cloud behind it and the horses were bathed in sweat, their heads still high even after hours of pulling the heavy coach in their wake. He stepped quickly to the sidewalk opposite and shoved his hands deeper in his pockets, rocking back on his heels while he waited. The weight of his holster pulled on his hips, and he tugged his pants up a little.

As the stage came to a halt, the horses snorted, dropped their heads low and sucked in deep breaths. It looked as though Stan had driven them harder than he normally did. He frowned and scratched at his nose. As used to the trip as they were, that was highly unusual.

A heavy-set old woman emerged from the coach, a handkerchief dabbing at her mouth. Her arm was supported by a greasy middle-aged fellow with a receding hairline and drooping mustache. He fussed over her, then stood aside as she barked orders at the boy who'd jumped from the driver's seat to unload the luggage.

Ed walked over. "Say, Peter, where's Galloway? And why'd you drive the horses so hard? He wouldn't be happy seein' you treat 'em that way…" His voice drifted off as he looked up and saw the blood-covered body of Stan Galloway tied to the back of the coach. "What in tarnation…?"

Peter rubbed his hands over his face. Dirty streaks ran from his eyes down both cheeks and off his chin. "We was robbed, Sheriff. They shot him and got away with most of the valuables. I didn't know what to do."

Ed rested a hand on the lad's back. "There now,

'course you didn't. You did good just gettin' the passengers here on your own. Go see if Sally has somethin' warm to soothe your throat, boy. You can come back out to take care of the horses after that." He watched Peter cross the street and amble into the Roan Horse Saloon. Sally Yancey the owner had a soft heart, and would give him a hearty meal and an ear to listen to his woes.

Ed ran his fingers over his mustache and turned to look at the dead body again. The first thing was to get the old man down from there and give him some dignity, but he'd need help.

Another woman stepped cautiously out of the coach, a gloved hand holding the door, her black damask gown sweeping the step behind her. She glanced around and caught sight of him, her hazel eyes masking whatever she might have felt—they were deep and warm, but if she'd been frightened by the attack, she didn't show it.

His heart thudded in his chest and his pulse raced at the sight of her. Her eyes seemed to burn into his, as though she saw who he was and could learn everything about him with one look. She was the most beautiful woman he'd ever seen, and around Coloma she really stood out. Most of the women there were either old and married or of ill repute, and all of them had experienced difficult lives that showed on their faces. A man couldn't help but pity them—them and the local men, most of whose worn faces showed they'd traveled a road or two themselves.

He removed his ten-gallon hat. "Er… Miss?" His tongue felt like it was tied in a knot, and his cheeks flamed.

She arched a single slim eyebrow at him. "Yes?"

"I'm Sheriff Edward Milton. Just wonderin', did you see what happened to Mr. Galloway here?"

Her hand went to her throat. "See it? Of course I did—I was sitting right inside the coach. I saw, heard and felt every last thing that happened."

He bit his tongue. She was feisty and given the fright she'd experienced, maybe a little hysterical. He decided to give her a bit of leeway. "I'm sorry to hear that, Miss…?"

"Miss Stout—Hattie Stout, from New York City."

He raised an eyebrow. She'd said her name as though he would recognize it. He wondered what in Heaven's name an elegant young woman like her was doing, apparently all alone, in a town like Coloma. "Do you think you might be able to recognize the ones who did it?"

She shook her head and sighed. "I'm afraid their faces were covered. They wore neckerchiefs pulled up over their mouths and noses, and hats were drawn down low. There were only three of them, if that helps."

He rubbed his chapped lips and frowned. He'd been after a trio of rascals for months. This was likely the same team that had been stealing payrolls and valuables from mines and ranches all over El Dorado County. No one yet had been able to give him a description or any information to help him catch the scoundrels. Well, they couldn't have gotten far yet. He'd find Peter and ask him for an account of where the attack happened, and with a posse of angry townsmen, maybe they'd be able to track the men down this time.

Ed tipped his hat and bid Miss Stout farewell, then marched across the street to the Roan Horse. He'd find help there to take care of the body, and likely a posse as well. He hated that there were outlaws in his county he'd been unable to apprehend—before they'd come along, his record had been stellar. He was the sheriff with the most arrests of wanted felons in all of California, and he wasn't about to let some two-bit hustlers take his reputation from him.

Chapter Two

Hattie watched a group of angry-looking men on horseback storm out of town, led by the disheveled sheriff she'd met earlier. She frowned and wiped her forehead. Even though it was only May, the heat of the California spring already had her bathed in sweat. Thank goodness it was almost sunset—she didn't know how much more of it she could take without passing out. She dreaded what summer would be like.

The sinking sun lit up the raw timber buildings of Coloma with pinks and oranges, bathing the landscape in a soft golden glow. Her legs ached from standing and the other passengers had long since left. She glanced around as townsfolk scurried by, staring at her as they passed. No doubt she stood out from the crowd of homespun weaves and ill-fitting gowns. She wrapped her arms around her thin frame, hoping to become invisible from the prying eyes of every passerby.

She wasn't used to standing on the street with nowhere to go. Where was the husband she'd travelled all this way to meet? He'd written in his last correspondence that he'd pick her up from the stagecoach—she hadn't considered the possibility he might not even have the decency to show up. Or perhaps something had happened to him since he last sent a telegram east? There was no way of knowing where he might be or how to find him. She should have asked more questions.

And now after the robbery, she didn't even have enough money to pay for a night in the seedy-looking hovel across the street—*The Roan Horse Saloon*, read the sign over the front door. She shivered and hugged herself tighter, then finally sat on the boardwalk next to her carpetbag.

A man was catapulted through the swinging front doors of the saloon, across the covered sidewalk and onto the road. He landed in a heap, the sound of whooping and catcalls followed him outside. She tucked her gown a little tighter around her legs, her pulse racing.

Oh, why had Father sent her here? Surely he could have found a better way to deal with the loss of the family fortune. And if only Frank Jones had followed through on his promise to marry her—they'd been engaged, for Heaven's sake! But apparently that had meant nothing to his parents, who'd insisted he break the agreement and marry his cousin instead. Something about keeping the bloodlines strong and the business in the family...

She'd cried when he told her he planned to submit to their wishes. She'd loved him and had spent many a night dreaming about their future life together. If he hadn't backed out, she'd be living in a fine house in New York City and everything would be just great. Instead she was stranded on the edge of civilization, alone. No one cared about her. What would become of her? Tears filled her eyes and the ache in her throat grew more than she could bear.

A pair of boots stopped in front of her, obscuring her view of the street. She raised her eyes slowly, taking in the grimy dungarees, low-slung holster with a silver pistol on either side, faded checked shirt and brown vest. The bearded face above a thick chest was one she recognized. His blue eyes twinkled above a black beard, and one chiseled cheek sported a dimple above a dark beard, and a half-grin that revealed a set of straight white teeth. "Sheriff Milton."

He set his hands to his hips and tilted his head to one side. "Miss Stout, wasn't it?"

She nodded and sniffed back the tears that threatened to break free.

"Ain't you meetin' someone?"

A single tear wound its way down her cheek and she slapped at the traitorous drip. "I am."

"Still not here, huh?"

With a shake of the head, she felt her nostrils flare. Had he returned to revel in her predicament? Surely if he were a gentleman, he wouldn't embarrass her further in her despair. "I thought you'd left town," she snapped.

He chewed on his lip a moment. "Just gettin' a posse together. We'll be leavin' shortly."

She frowned and stared at the toe of her boot. Why wouldn't he just go away and leave her alone?

"What's his name? This person you're meetin'—perhaps I know him." He shifted his hat to one side to scratch his head, then returned it to its place.

She sniffed again. "If you must know, though I can't say it's any of your business, the man's name is Jack Miller. He's to be my husband."

The sheriff's eyebrows shot skyward. "I know Jack. He's a right…interestin' fella. You're gonna marry him?"

The look in his eyes made her heart drop. She knew it—her husband-to-be was a lout, a good-for-nothing. It was her worst nightmare come true. She took a long, slow breath, waiting for her heart rate to slow before she spoke again. "Do you know where I can find him?"

"Why'd you come all the way from New York City to marry Jack Miller?"

"Because…well, because my family lost its fortune and my father sent me west as a mail-order bride. I had no choice in the matter. I can assure you, if I had, I wouldn't have chosen this God-forsaken hovel as my place of residence!" That was rude and she knew it, but she felt as though she might throw up at any moment.

She truly didn't know what to do next. Unless her fiancé showed up soon, she'd spend the night on the street—and by the quality of people spilling out of the various saloons and bawdy houses that lined its edges before the sun had even set, she knew she would be in danger. Her eyes flooded with unshed tears and she dropped her gaze to the road so he wouldn't see the depth of her misery.

"A mail-order bride, huh? Well then, I guess we'd better see if we can find the lucky fella. Though I think it's best you get off the street for now. Have you had anythin' to eat?"

She shook her head as her lower lip trembled.

He grinned. "All right, then—come with me. I was just 'bout to go over to the Roan, so you might as well join me. You cain't very well spend the night out here, sittin' on your luggage."

"Thank you." She stood and smoothed down her

skirts. The first star sparkled overhead as she trudged across the street after the sheriff, who had slung her carpetbag over his shoulder and pulled her trunk behind him.

She paused when he pushed through the swinging doors into the saloon. She'd never been inside an establishment like it in her life, and knew Father wouldn't approve. But the sheriff didn't stop or look back over his shoulder, and she was afraid she'd lose sight of him. With a deep breath, she pushed open the doors and stepped inside.

A bar lined the far wall, and several ragged patrons leaned against it. An upright piano sat in a far corner, and a woman dressed only in pantaloons and a corset sat on its lid, her legs crossed and suspenders holding up a pair of worn stockings. She smiled at Hattie in puzzlement, and Hattie's eyes widened. The sheriff disappeared through an archway beside the piano, and she scurried after him.

The next room held a series of small square tables, most full of men and a few women, eating steaming food from faded plates. Hattie wove quickly between the tables and caught up to the sheriff, just as he set her trunk and carpetbag against the back wall and settled into a chair at an empty table. She sat in a chair across from him, her ankles crossed demurely and her hands clenched tightly together in her lap.

He laughed and raised an eyebrow. "Relax, honey. It ain't that bad."

Her eyes narrowed and she unclenched her hands. Honestly, she wasn't sure how she was supposed to relax in a place like this. She only hoped Jack Miller would come soon and she could forget this place ever existed.

"What do you wanna eat, then?" he asked as a waitress wiped down the newly empty table beside them and flashed him a grin. He smiled in return, then turned back to Hattie.

"Um… I'm not sure. What do you recommend?"

"The johnnycakes are good, and the mutton. I think I'll get the beef stew, though—it fills the emptiness."

"Fine, I'll have the stew as well. Thank you."

The waitress nodded and hurried off toward what must have been the kitchen. A delicious aroma of meats, bread and other good food wafted from the door into which she disappeared, along with the clanging noise of pots and pans.

Hattie's eyes flitted over the faces of the other patrons and she soon realized they weren't paying her any mind. People were deep in conversation or engrossed with their meals, and after the first curious glances they'd returned to them. She took a deep breath, then exhaled slowly, willing her heart rate to slow to normal.

"I hain't seen Jack in town lately. You're sure he was expectin' you today?" The sheriff crossed his arms, the star fixed to the outside of his vest shining in the lamplight.

She nodded. "Yes, he was expecting me. Though we didn't discuss what to do if he was waylaid."

He pressed his lips together and leaned forward. "I tell you what. If he hasn't showed up by the time we're done eatin', I'll see what I can do to find you a place to spend the night. A young lady such as yourself shouldn't be left alone in a place like this—not after dark."

She felt a rush of gratitude for this man—he'd never

met her before and yet had already done more for her than any of her friends in New York had been willing to. "Thank you, sir."

The waitress returned with their meals, setting a large dish of stew in front of each of them. "Thanks, Sally," the sheriff said, adding some salt to his plate. "Hey, you got any spare rooms tonight for this young lady?"

The woman set her hands on her ample hips and eyed Hattie suspiciously. "I might."

"It'd be a favor for me, you understand." The sheriff took a spoonful of stew and chewed with eyes closed. "Mmmm…delicious as always, Sally." His eyes flicked opened and he grinned at their hostess.

Sally's eyes were still fixed accusingly on Hattie. "Thank ya, Sheriff. Well, if it's a favor for ya, course she can stay. Ya saved me and the Roan too many times to count, so I'll look after her as if she were my own." The woman pulled a dish towel from her apron and turned to wipe down a table.

"Thank you," Hattie called to her retreating back. Tears pricked at her eyes and she blinked them away. At least she wouldn't have to sleep on her luggage in the street like a common vagabond. She felt suddenly famished, and the aroma of the stew made her mouth water in anticipation. She lifted a spoonful of stew to her mouth, and her eyes widened in surprise. It tasted delightful, and in no time her stomach was satisfied by the hearty fare.

Well…maybe Coloma wouldn't be so bad. But where was her intended?

The sun peeked around the thin draperies and slapped Hattie across the face. She groaned and rolled over in the bed. The rustle of the straw tick made her eyes fly open and she sat up with a start, her gaze darting around the room. Where was she?

Then she remembered—the Roan Horse. She was in a small, shabby room above a saloon in a mining town somewhere near Hell. Her heart thudded and her head grew light. What would the day bring?

There was a sharp knock at the door and she jumped. "Yes, who is it?" she called out, as she stood, put her housecoat on and cinched the tie around her waist.

"Miss Stout?" Sally's gravelly voice sounded under the door. "Jack Miller's here to see ya. Should I tell him ya'll be down shortly?"

Hattie's eyes grew round. Jack was here, finally! He hadn't abandoned her after all. She wasn't sure whether to be glad or panic, but either way, she'd have to get dressed. "Yes, I'll be down as soon as I can!" she called back.

As Sally's footsteps faded down the hall, Hattie got to work. She washed up quickly using the chipped ceramic washbowl in the corner, and dressed in a cornflower-blue frock with lace-trimmed sleeves and neckline. She laced up her boots, brushed her hair until it shone in the looking glass and fixed it into a chignon. She regarded her reflection with satisfaction, then repacked her trunk and headed downstairs, lugging her baggage behind her.

When she reached the bottom of the narrow staircase, she saw a man leaning against the bar with his ankles crossed and a black Stetson on his head. He was spinning a glass of amber liquid around on top of the bar, the drink shining in the sunlight that streamed through the swinging doors.

He looked up and caught her gaze with a half-smile that made his cheeks dimple. He ran a hand over his beard and looked her slowly up and down, the smile stretching further. Then he straightened purposefully, lifted the glass to his lips and downed it in one gulp.

She took a deep breath as he made his way over to her. "You must be Hattie," he drawled. "I'm Jack Miller. Pleased to meet ya." He extended a hand, took hers and kissed the back of her white glove.

Jack Miller didn't cut an impressive figure—his clothing was old and stained, and he smelled of sweat, tobacco and livestock. But her skin tingled beneath the fabric of her glove and she felt her cheeks flush. "Yes, I'm Hattie Stout. It's a pleasure to meet you as well, Mr. Miller."

His gaze found hers, and the look in his eyes made her swallow hard. "Sorry I wasn't here to meet yer stage last evenin'. Somethin' held me up, but I got here quick as I could."

She nodded. "Never mind. Sheriff Milton secured me a room upstairs for the night. I didn't have the money to pay for accommodation since our stage was held up by outlaws before we arrived."

His face blanched and his gaze dropped to the floor. "That so? Sorry to hear that. Lemme get them bags of yours." He reached for her luggage and lifted it easily in his strong arms. "Let's get on over to the court-house—we can get married and be on our way. I got a cabin a few miles outside town, and I'd like to be back by lunch time so I can feed the livestock afore dark."

She nodded as her heart thudded. They were to marry right away? She supposed it made sense, but she hadn't expected it—she'd hoped they'd get to know each other a little while before tying the knot. Since she didn't really have other options, though, it likely wouldn't make any difference. She followed him out the swinging doors and into the bright sunshine of another California spring day.

The courthouse was two streets over and a few blocks down. The town itself wasn't much—a settlement of a few hundred people overshadowed by the rolling hills that were pockmarked by a long, ugly series of mines. The short squat courthouse, built of stone with dusty glass windows, stood in the center of it all.

Hattie struggled to keep up with her fiancé, who set a brisk pace as he strode down the street, eliciting wary glances from most he passed. Some men doffed their hats to him, but the women scurried out of his way and ushered their children to the side away from him. She barely noticed, her heart in her throat over the idea of tying herself for the rest of her days to a man she'd just met—a man who smelled of sweat and whiskey and looked as though he hadn't bathed in a month.

She choked back a sob and broke into a jog behind him.

Chapter Three

Ed pushed through the swinging doors of the Roan Horse and sauntered across the dust-covered floor toward the bar. Sally stood behind it, wiping a glass dry between her stubby hands. "Hey there, Sheriff. How're ya doin' today?" She smiled at him, revealing a gap where her bottom front teeth should have been.

"Howdy, Sally. I'm fine, thanks. And you?"

She nodded. "Well as can be expected. What can I do for ya?"

He took off his hat and scanned the room. "Just lookin' in on Miss Stout. Thought I might see how she's farin'."

Sally set the dry glass on the counter and frowned. "She seemed fine when she left. Though I hafta admit, I'm surprised she came west to marry that lowlife Jack Miller. Pity for her, is all I can say."

Ed's heart thudded and his eyebrows flew sky-high. "She left already?"

"Uh-huh." Sally reached for another clean glass.

"With him?"

"He's her fiancé, ain't he?"

Ed slammed his ten-gallon hat back on his head. "Well, then, I guess that's the end of that."

Sally shot him a curious look. "End of what?"

"Oh, nothing. Dadgummit." He spun on his heel and strode from the saloon, thoughts buzzing through his head. He couldn't stand that Hattie Stout was marrying a man like Jack Miller. It was her prerogative to wed whomever she pleased, of course, but a man like that…well, he didn't deserve someone as beautiful and refined as her. Oh, she'd be a handful, all right. But a handful Ed would be willing to live with given half the chance.

That didn't matter one jot anymore, seeing as how she'd already pledged herself to another man—even a two-bit hustler like Jack Miller.

When Hattie reached the courthouse, she noticed a circle of white-winged butterflies fluttering around a bush by the porch rail. She paused a moment, her pulse racing and breathing jagged, to study them. They were beautiful and peaceful and paid no mind to the turmoil going on around them in the world. She lifted a hand toward one as if to cup it in her palm, but it flapped its delicate wings and shied out of reach.

"Ya comin'?" barked Jack, his eyebrows drawn low over dark eyes.

She shuddered, lifted her skirts in one hand and skipped up the stairs to where he stood, holding the door for her. He wasn't even puffing after toting her heavy bags so quickly from the saloon to the courthouse. His muscular arms bulged beneath his shirt sleeves, which were rolled up to his elbows, exposing skin weathered by hours in the sun.

"Are we to be married by a minister?" she asked, almost in a whisper.

He shook his head, one short sharp motion, and frowned. "Nope."

Her breath caught in her throat and she closed her eyes. When she opened them again, Jack was gone, and she could hear voices behind the closed door. Her luggage lay on the porch beside a wicker chair, which she sank down into with a sigh.

Soon Jack returned with an anxious-looking man whose spectacles sat low on the end of his long, pointed nose. "So can you marry us?" Jack asked, tipping his hat forward to scratch at his head.

The man nodded, then blinked. "Miss Stout, is it?"

"Yes, I'm Hattie Stout." She stood and offered him her hand.

He took it and gave it a limp shake. "Pleased to make your acquaintance. I'm Tom Small, the resident justice of the peace. Follow me, if you please." He turned and went back through the door, holding it open for them to pass through.

They entered a room with a sturdy wooden desk covered in neat stacks of paper. He hurried around to the other side of the desk and pulled open a drawer. Extracting a sheet of paper, he peered down his nose through the spectacles to assess its contents, then pressed his thin lips together with a grunt. "This is it. All right, then, let's get to it."

The vows they repeated were perfunctory and brief. When he reached the end, Mr. Small in his high monotone announced that Jack could kiss his bride. Hattie's heart lurched as her new husband leaned in and planted his lips on hers with a wet smack.

When he pulled away, she noticed for the first time a scar running down the side of his face and into his beard. She hadn't stood close enough to him until that moment to see it. Her heart thundered and her mouth fell open in dismay. His black beard and dark eyes flashed before her eyes—along with a brown neckerchief pulled up high over his nose and mouth.

Mr. Small hurried out to finalize their paperwork, announcing his intention to return shortly. As soon as he was gone, Hattie gasped and pulled back with a cry.

Jack watched her reaction, puzzled. "What? What's wrong?"

"You! You're the outlaw who robbed the stage! I recognize your scar. No wonder you let me keep my luggage—it was you. You knew I was coming here to marry you!"

His eyes widening, he slapped a hand over her mouth. "Quiet now!" he hissed. "You're my wife, whether ya like it or not. So you'd better keep them thoughts to yourself if you know what's good for ya—"

She bit the palm of his hand. He let go with a shout and pulled his hand back to slap her, but she ducked around him and ran with all her might out the door, almost bowling Mr. Small over as he rounded the corner with the marriage certificate in his long, bony fingers. "Mrs. Miller?" he cried in alarm. "Where are you going? I've got your certificate… Mrs. Miller!"

She paid him no mind, running pell-mell across the foyer, out the front door, down the porch stairs and into the street. She gasped as her corset stays dug into her sides, but kept on, her legs pumping and elbows flailing. A glance back over her shoulder showed he hadn't followed her, and relief washed over her, but she didn't stop.

Thud!—Hattie ran headlong into a broad, and very hard, chest. She sank toward the ground, her knees buckling beneath her, even as she felt strong hands grasp her arms and lift her back to her feet.

Disappointed in finding Hattie gone from the Roan, Ed headed for his office. But as he turned a corner, a woman ran smack into him. She acted like she might faint, and he caught her in his arms, then realized who it was. "Whoa there! Miss Stout, are you all right?"

Her eyelids flickered and she exhaled sharply. "Sheriff! I'm so glad I found you." She took another breath. "It's Jack! He's the robber!"

"What?" He frowned. "What are you talking about?"

"Jack Miller robbed the stagecoach!"

His eyes widened as she fell against his chest, clutching at his waistcoat. He set his hands under her arms and lifted her gently out of the way. "Where is he now?"

She lifted a shaking hand, pointing back the way she'd come. "I just left him at the courthouse."

Ed nodded. "Go back to the Roan Horse and stay with Sally—tell her I said so. I'll check on you as soon as I've caught the scoundrel." He stepped past her and ran to the courthouse, leaping up the stairs in two long bounds and pushing through the door. "Tom! Tom, where are you?"

Tom Small peered out his office door anxiously, then came into the entryway to greet the sheriff, twisting his hands together in front of him. "Sheriff, good to see you. You know, the strangest thing just hap—"

"Where is he?" barked Ed, his eyes darting around.

"I suppose you mean Jack Miller?"

"Yes, I do." Ed frowned in frustration and rested his hands on his hips.

Tom pushed his spectacles back up the bridge of his nose and blinked. "He just left—followed his wife out the door. No idea why they were in such a hurry—I was only gone a few moments to get the stamp for their marriage certificate. When I came back, she nearly knocked me to the ground on her way out. He ran out after her."

"Thanks!" Ed called over his shoulder as he rushed back through the door. Likely Jack, having been found out, was already on his way out of town. He had a head start, but he wouldn't get away easily if Ed had anything to say about it. He sprinted to the stables behind his office, where his chestnut gelding Fire stood munching on a mouthful of hay, saddled and ready to go.

"*Oye*, boss." A short, stocky man wearing a tan Stetson stepped from the shadows—Leandro "Lee" Perez, one of Ed's deputies. "Where you headed?"

Ed leaped onto Fire's back and gathered the reins in his hands. "Someone fingered Jack Miller as one of the stagecoach thieves. He's fleeing town right now."

Lee ran back into the stable, calling over his shoulder. "*Dios mio!* I'm coming with you!"

The two of them rode out of town together moments later, hot on Jack Miller's trail. Ed grinned—thanks to that girl from New York, he'd finally caught a break in the case.

* * *

Hattie couldn't move for a minute, just stood in the street gasping for breath, tugging at her stays and fanning her face with both hands. But the sheriff didn't reappear. He'd told her to go back to the Roan Horse, and she supposed there wasn't anything else for it but to do as he'd said. She frowned—she'd hoped never to set foot in the place again, but she didn't really have much of a choice.

Looking up and down the street didn't provide any better options—a paint-chipped mercantile, two more saloons, a dance hall, a livery and a couple of other businesses she couldn't identify from where she stood. Finally she pushed her wayward hair behind her ears and staggered across the street to the Roan Horse.

Sally looked up from her mop in surprise when Hattie walked into the saloon. "Well, lookie here—didn't 'spect to see ya again so soon. Ya forget somethin'?"

Hattie frowned, then sighed. "No, I didn't. But the sheriff told me to come back here, and I do need a place to stay, again. Any chance I could get my room back? I'd be willing to work to pay my way."

Sally laughed. "Work? Do ya even know how to work?"

Hattie thought she should feel insulted, but she didn't have the energy. "No, I don't suppose I do. I've never really had to. But I don't have anywhere else to go, all my money was stolen, my things…" She blanched—everything she owned save what she was wearing was still sitting on the courthouse porch! And she couldn't exactly go back there—what if Jack was waiting for her? "…anyway, I'm desperate. So I'll do what you need me to do as best I can."

Sally stopped mopping and rested the handle against the bar behind her. Hands on her hips, she surveyed Hattie through narrowed eyes. "That so? What happened to that good-for-nothin' fiancé of yers? Ditch ya at the altar?"

Hattie shook her head as she felt her anger rise. "No. I ran away after I realized he'd robbed the stagecoach I came here on."

That got Sally's attention. "Well! You sure have had an adventure, ain't ya?" She sighed, a little more sympathetic now. "All right, ya can stay a while. But ya'll be workin' hard for it—I don't run no charity. You can start by mopping this whole floor." She lifted the mop by the handle and held it out to Hattie.

Hattie took it with a grateful smile. "Thank you, Sally. I appreciate it more than you know."

Sally shrugged. "We'll see." She bustled from the room, shaking her head.

Hattie watched her leave, then began mopping. As she did, she wondered how she could get her trunk and carpetbag from the court house. It was possible Jack Miller, the cad, had taken them already, but there was nothing she could do right now about it. Once she'd finished whatever chores Sally had for her, she'd go back and fetch them—if they were still there.

Ed strode into the Roan Horse at lunch time in a foul mood. He'd been too late to catch Jack Miller—the varmint was probably out of town by the time Sally had run into him. The only bright side was that now he knew the identity of one of the stage robbers...provided Hattie had been right about him.

For now, he wanted to check on her and grab a bite

to eat. She was likely safe and sound in Sally's hands. There were a million other things he could be attending to around town: horse thieves, cattle rustlers, altercations between ranchers about property lines. But here he was, checking in on a New York girl he'd only just met. Well, at least he could justify it if anyone asked— she *was* a witness to a stagecoach robbery…

He shook his head and stopped at the bar, leaning his elbows on the counter. "Hey, Sally. How's it goin'?" He took off his hat and set it on the bar beside him.

Sally sauntered over to serve him, a dish towel slung over one broad shoulder. "Good, thanks, Sheriff. How 'bout you?"

He groaned. "Whiskey, please."

"That good, huh?" With a deft flick of the wrist, she poured him a glass.

He grabbed it and gulped it down in one mouthful. "That bad. So where's Miss Stout?" Sally tipped her head toward the door to the dining room, and he put his hat back on and nodded. "Thanks."

"Always a pleasure, Sheriff," said Sally to his back.

The dining room lunch crowd was sparse, with empty seats throughout. He spotted Hattie immediately, carrying an armful of dirty dishes toward the kitchen. She'd donned an apron over her fine blue gown. Her dark hair hung in messy tendrils around her pale face, her mouth was pulled into a tight pink line and her cheeks were flushed.

He located an empty table, pulled out a chair and lowered himself into it with a sigh. He was tired after the long gallop to Slot Creek, where they'd lost Jack's tracks. After an hour of searching, he and Lee had given up. His whole body ached, and he slapped his hat down on the table and combed his fingers through his sweat-soaked hair.

Hattie returned from the kitchen, carrying a tray of full plates which she set down at various tables. Just as she passed a group of four grimy miners with more than a few empty beer glasses in front of them, one of them leaned over and slapped her on the rear with a loud guffaw. His companions burst into laughter along with him, and another man grabbed Hattie and pulled her into his lap with a laugh. Hattie tried to stand, but the man pulled her back.

Ed's eyes narrowed and he stood to his feet. He reached the men in three long strides and stared down at them, his hand resting on his holster. "What's goin' on here?"

The miners' laughter faded and they shifted uneasily in their seats. The one who'd corralled Hattie released her. "Just…havin' a bit of fun, Sheriff," he mumbled as she jumped away.

Ed's blood pounded through his veins and his head swam. He reached for the man's collar and hauled him to his feet. "That's no way to treat a lady," he growled.

"I'm sorry," he simpered, his face turning red.

The man's friends stood slowly, fists clenching. "C'mon now, Sheriff—no need to cause a stink about it," one huffed.

Ed dropped the man he was holding, lifted his elbow in a flash and felled the speaker with a crack to the chin, then brought his fist up to connect with the first fellow's nose, making it spurt with blood. The bleeder ran from the saloon in a howl of agony. The other two followed quickly, trailed by the second speaker, who was still woozy but not inclined to hang around and recover.

Ed turned to Hattie in concern. He strode to her side, lifted a hand toward her cheek, then let it fall to his side as his own cheeks warmed. "Are you all right, Miss Stout?"

She caught his hand as it fell and held it between hers. "Thank you, Sheriff."

His skin tingled beneath her touch, and his gaze fixed on her wide hazel eyes as his pulse raced. "You're welcome," he croaked. He cleared his throat. "I…hope you weren't injured."

She shook her head and lifted a hand to flutter at her throat. "No, but I don't know what might have happened if you hadn't been here."

He tipped his hat. "So long as you're well, then. I just came by to let you know I wasn't able to track down your intended. He escaped—for now, anyway. But we'll catch up with him soon enough." He dropped her hand and turned to walk away.

Her voice stopped him dead in his tracks. "Alas, he's not my intended anymore, Sheriff. He's my husband."

His eyes flew wide and he swallowed hard as he turned back. "Husband?"

Red circles flared on her cheeks as she nodded. "I'm afraid we were married before I realized who he was."

His heart dropped. He couldn't stand to think of her being married to that cad. She didn't deserve it, and Jack sure didn't deserve her. It didn't matter to him one way or the other—even if she were available, it wasn't likely she'd be interested in a small-town lawman. But it unsettled him, more than he liked to admit.

Ed nodded, forced a smile and marched out of the saloon. This day just kept going downhill, like a horseless wagon.

Chapter Four

Hattie's shift in the restaurant was finally over. She pulled her aching feet out of her boots, kicked them aside and laid back on the thin bed, the straw rustling beneath her.

She squinted against the afternoon sunlight. The room she shared with Daisy Sweeney, a "sporting woman", was narrow but well-lit from the single window high on the wall above her bed. She'd be waiting tables again in two hours' time when the supper shift began, but for now she had time to rest and relax.

A rap on the door startled her. She sat up with a sigh, running her hands over her disheveled hair. "Yes, come in."

The door creaked open and Sally poked her head in, blonde curls framing her plump, lined face. She sidled through the opening, her eyes narrowed. "How long ya been workin' here now?" she asked, one eyebrow arched.

Hattie stood quickly, smoothing her skirts. "A few weeks. Why?"

"More like six weeks, ain't it?"

"I guess so." Truth be told, she'd lost track.

"Well, it's time you had a bit of fun."

Hattie tipped her head to one side. "Fun?"

"Yeah. There's a picnic over at the church this afternoon. You and Daisy should go."

Hattie chewed the inside of her cheek. A picnic? That did sound fun. "But I'm supposed to work..."

"Never mind that—I'll cover for ya. You're young, you should enjoy yerself. I've enjoyed myself plenty—I don't need no more fun." Sally chuckled as she edged back out the doorway. "Get dressed—Daisy'll be up soon and you can go."

Hattie slumped back down on the bed, lay on top of the covers, tucked her arms behind her head and smiled. A picnic. She hadn't been to a social engagement since she left New York, and just the idea of it had her pulse racing.

She'd been living and working at the Roan Horse for weeks and still her husband roamed free. The sheriff checked in with her a few times per week, but he hadn't been able to catch Jack Miller or his still-unknown accomplices. At first she'd been afraid he'd return for her. Then she'd been terrified Sally would toss her out on the streets when she didn't have a natural gift for saloon work.

But as time passed, she began to adapt to this new life, and the danger seemed to have passed. She'd settled into a routine and become a reasonably proficient waitress, at least according to Sally. All she wanted now was to work long enough to earn her passage back home. It was what she focused on every day when she mopped the saloon floor, washed the piles of dirty dishes or fended off yet another handsy miner.

Daisy barreled through the door, tugging at the neckline of her dress, her ample bosoms spilling out over the top of the fabric. She grinned and kicked Hattie's bed, and Hattie sat up with a groan. "Am I to get no rest in this place?"

"Did you hear? We're gonna go to the town picnic." Daisy skipped in a circle, one hand to her mouth and her pinky finger raised high. "My oh my, won't we be grand?" She burst into giggles, her stomach shaking.

Hattie rolled her eyes. "Yes, indeed—cracked hands, stained house dress and all." She dabbed at a rather large stain on her bodice with a grimace. She could at least change her clothes—thankfully her bags were still at the courthouse when she got back that horrible day, and she'd hauled them to the Roan herself. But now, most of her dresses looked as bad as the one she was currently wearing.

"Never mind all that. The *sheriff* will be there." Daisy raised an eyebrow and grinned, revealing large white teeth.

"What do you mean by that?"

"You know full well what I mean. I never saw the man visit the saloon so often as he has since you've been here. And every time he comes, he makes sure to bump into you, or just plain asks to see ya. He's smitten, is what he is. Smitten!" She threw her head back and laughed.

Hattie stalked to the looking glass and fiddled with her hair. "I don't know what you mean. He updates me on their search for Jack, that's all. I can assure you, Sheriff Milton is no more in love with me than he is with Sally. Quite possibly less." She pushed a hairpin back into place and took a long slow breath.

She honestly wasn't sure if she was telling the truth or not. She'd noticed the sheriff's attentiveness to her, but had shrugged it off. After having her heart broken in New York, then marrying an outlaw, she wanted to stay well away from men, the handsome sheriff included. She had to focus if she wanted to get home again—focus and work hard. And she wouldn't let anyone, not even the tall, broad-shouldered lawman, get in the way of that.

Ed lifted a hay bale from the wagon bed and carried it over his head to set in the field beside the small white chapel that sat on the rise overlooking Coloma. The structure shone in the summer sun, and he could feel a trickle of sweat winding its way down his back while he worked.

His two deputies were helping him set up the annual picnic. Hans Bergman and Lee Perez's button-down shirts stuck to their skin in the dry heat. Lee shifted his Stetson back from his head and wiped the sweat from his brow. "I think we're about done," he said, shooting a hopeful grin at his boss.

Hans sighed and slouched down onto a bale. "Phew! I bet folks'll be glad it's an evening picnic with this heat."

"Yeah, the sun's about to set—everythin' will cool off then." Ed wiped his face dry with his kerchief. "You fellas go get yourselves a drink of lemonade. I can see Sally's already set up the drinks over yonder."

Hans and Lee happily complied, hurrying to where Sally stood, behind a table with a large punch bowl filled to the brim with ice-cold lemonade and slices of fresh lemon. Ed licked his lips and followed. He wondered if Hattie would make it, and was trying to think of a way to ask Sally without being teased. She'd given him no respite in recent weeks when he'd visit the saloon in hopes of speaking with the young woman. Lately he'd stayed away—he hadn't seen her in at least a week.

He'd been feeling the frustration build lately over the search for Jack Miller, Hattie's no-good husband. The scoundrel had managed to stay just out of reach. It didn't seem to matter how often they put together a posse and went after him, he was always a step ahead of them. They'd found his camps twice in recent weeks, once even with warm water in a pot over the fire, the embers still glowing. But no sign of Jack or his friends, and no trails to follow for more than a mile.

Ed so wanted to catch the cur—and not just because of the robberies, though that would be reason enough. He'd finally admitted to himself that he was intent on bringing the man in for Hattie's sake. He didn't know how it would help, but somehow it seemed it might.

He should really just forget all about her. From what Sally told him, Hattie's plan was to save enough money to go back to New York and her family first thing. Sally didn't mind—she'd only given Hattie a job out of the kindness of her heart. In her words, the girl was about as bad a waitress as one could imagine.

Ed reached the lemonade table and dipped himself a large cup, downing it in three gulps. His gaze traveled over the picnic area. He had to admit, it looked downright pretty with lanterns around the space, picnic rugs dotting the dusty ground and tables and chairs set up against the side of the white chapel.

The first wagons arrived, and he wandered down

to meet them. People were showing up on foot as well, mostly folks who lived in town—the farmers and ranchers traveled by wagon. By the time he reached level ground, they were parking and settling their horses with feed bags, amidst a buzz of activity.

Daisy and Hattie appeared by his side, and his heart lurched. Daisy offered him a gap-toothed grin beneath her white bonnet, and Hattie smiled demurely from under a wide-brimmed blue one. "Good evening, Sheriff," cried Daisy in her Irish brogue, extending her pudgy hand.

"Daisy, Hattie, how are you?" He took off his hat and kissed their hands. He longed to kiss more than just Hattie's delicate hand—his cheeks flushed with warmth at her touch.

As Daisy dragged Hattie off toward the lemonade and plates of sandwiches that had been laid out, Hattie glanced at him over her shoulder, and the depth of her wide hazel eyes made his breath catch in his throat. Why did she affect him the way she did? He had to pull himself together. He couldn't let himself fall apart over a woman married to an outlaw, who would be riding the train back east at the first opportunity.

Ed was the sheriff of Coloma and he'd worked hard for the privilege. He couldn't afford to lose his heart to a debutante from New York, no matter how much she made it race.

Hattie sipped lemonade as townsfolk and ranchers descended on the picnic area. A band next to the chapel, two men with violins and one with a harmonium, began playing. Her foot tapped to the music, and she grinned as various couples converged onto a flat, dusty square of land and began to dance.

Daisy lurched into the chair beside her with a grunt, a plate full of victuals balanced in one hand, a cup of coffee in the other. "Ye get something to eat yet?" she asked between mouthfuls.

Hattie shook her head. "Not yet. I'm just enjoying the dancing. It feels so wonderful to be outside on a gorgeous night like this. Would you look at those stars—they're stunning! They light up the entire landscape..."

Daisy chuckled through a mouthful of ham and bread. "Ye're quite the poet, Hattie Stout."

"It's Miller," replied Hattie reluctantly. "Hattie Miller."

"If ye says so, lass. But surely you're not gonna keep his name, are you?"

"I don't know." Hattie felt a lump form in her throat that made it hard to speak. "I don't know what to do or think."

"Well, never mind all that tonight. We're gonna have some fun. Did ye see some of the blokes out here? Right handsome fellers." Daisy set her plate on the chair as she stood, dabbed at her mouth with a handkerchief and shoved it into her skirt pocket with a grin. "I'm gonna go find me someone to dance with. Watch me food, will you?" Waving goodbye to Hattie, she headed toward the dancers.

Hattie watched her leave, crossing her ankles in front of her. It felt rather lonely to sit on her own watching the groups and couples dotted around the field having such a grand time.

A shadow fell over her and she glanced up to see

Sheriff Milton standing there. She was taller than aver-
age, but he made her feel downright petite. He looked
at her with a half-grin on his handsome face. "Care to
dance, Miss Stout?"

She wanted to correct him about her name, but the
words wouldn't form. Her cheeks flamed and she gave
a quick nod of her head, then raised her hand to him.
He took it and she stood to follow him.

When they reached the rest of the couples, the song
wound to a finish and everyone stood around, a little
out of breath, waiting for the music to begin again. It
was a slow waltz this time, and the sheriff gently pulled
her close. She arched an eyebrow in surprise—he was
graceful despite his size, especially for a lawman from
a frontier mining town. Where had he learned to dance
like that?

The ground seemed to fly by beneath their feet and
the world spun around them. She found herself smiling
before she realized what she was doing. He had one
hand on her back, the other holding hers firmly, and
his eyes were fixed on hers. She'd never noticed before
how blue they were and how they crinkled around the
edges when he smiled. The music faded into the back-
ground, along with everything else around her. "Where
did you learn to dance, Sheriff?"

His eyes sparkled. "I haven't always lived in Coloma, Miss Stout."

"Oh? Where are you from?"

"Staunton, Virginia, originally. My aunt taught me
to dance, preparing me for society. I never ended up in
society as she deemed it, but it's still served me well."

Hattie thought so too. She didn't want this dance to
end. She didn't want to go back to the cramped room

she shared with Daisy, whose snoring would wake the dead; didn't want to work her fingers to the bone tomorrow in the saloon. She only wanted this moment, this dance, this man, forever.

Chapter Five

Hattie woke to the sunlight streaming in through the thin curtains, groaned and rolled over in her narrow bed. Her neck was stiff and her feet ached dully from the dance. She and the sheriff had danced for as long as they could stand, stopping only to eat. They'd sat comfortably side by side on a picnic blanket and discussed their families and lives before moving to Coloma. She'd told him all about her father's fall from grace and her journey west as a mail-order bride.

Their discussion made her ponder her time in the West. It wasn't all a nightmare—she'd made friends she'd never have thought she would. The love she felt for Daisy and even her surly boss Sally ran deeper than anything she'd felt for the friends she had back home.

Then there was Sheriff Ed Milton—the thought of leaving him behind made her throat ache. He'd always been so kind to her. The first time she met him, she'd considered him a rough-necked cowboy. But time had changed her opinion of him, and though she wanted nothing more than to return home, she couldn't help a twinge of regret at leaving him behind.

A sound outside caught her attention—someone was shuffling by the door? She was used to all kinds of noises—living above a saloon, people came and went by her room at all hours of the day and night. Daisy went in and out of their room at odd times as well. But this sound was different from what she'd grown accustomed to. She stood with a yawn and shuffled in bare feet over to the door, easing it open.

She remembered the first time she'd realized that Daisy was what her mother had once referred to as a "soiled dove." She'd been shocked beyond measure, her eyes wide as saucers. But Daisy had just laughed it off and told her she'd find herself in the same situation soon. "Ye'll be just like me, if Sally has her way. Everyone starts out in the dinin' room, waitin' tables. But stay here long enough and ye'll be entertainin' the men before ye know it."

That was the moment Hattie had vowed to herself to only stay long enough to save money for train fare. She'd never be pushed into selling herself the way Daisy and the other women in the saloon had.

She peered out and saw an empty hall, turned her head to look in the other direction and gasped when she saw Daisy seated against the wall, her head resting on her bent knees. One eye was blackened, and there was an ugly red welt down her cheek. Her clothing was torn, her skin exposed all the way down to her stomach on one side. "Daisy!" she cried, rushing out the door to kneel by her friend. "What's wrong? What happened?"

Daisy glanced up at her with streaks of tears running down her dirty face. She sobbed when she saw Hattie and knuckled her eyes.

"Who did this to you?" asked Hattie, anger flaring. But Daisy just shook her head and kept sobbing.

Hattie helped her to her feet, bundled her into their room and kicked the door closed behind them, then helped her to her bed. Daisy buried her face in a blanket, and Hattie lifted her feet onto the bed, unlaced her boots and tucked her in. She poured a cup of water from the pitcher beside the washbowl and passed it to her friend.

Daisy hiccupped, then gulped a great mouthful of water, her hands shaking around the cup. The sobbing soon subsided. Hattie sat beside Daisy on the bed and rested a hand on her arm.

"What happened to you?" she whispered, frowning thunderously.

Daisy took a deep breath, rubbed her eyes, then gasped at the pain and exhaled shakily. "It's nothing. I'm fine. I shouldn't have poked fun…it's just, ye know, I can't help meself sometimes. I joke around, tease a bit. Well, I guess this feller didn't have a sense of humor…" She forced a wry smile, then collapsed into a fresh bout of tears.

"One of the men you…see…did this to you?" Hattie's heart thudded and her cheeks flamed. Something had to be done about this. It wasn't right for anyone to be treated this way, certainly not the fun-loving friend she'd grown to care so much about over the past weeks.

"Don't fret o'er me." Daisy opened the drawer beside her bed, tugged out a clean handkerchief and blew her nose loudly into it. "I'll be fine—I've survived worse, I'll tell ye that. It was me own fault—sometimes I forget me place. Sally won't be pleased when she hears about it. She'll say I'm drivin' the men away and they won't come back if I make 'em upset. Oh, what if she throws me out this time? She's threatened before. This could be the final straw…" She sniffled and covered her face with the handkerchief, dabbing at her eyes.

"I can't believe Sally would do that," Hattie argued. "I mean, she lets *me* stay. She's got a soft heart—she wouldn't make you go unless you wanted to. And please don't say it's your fault—there's no excuse for any man to treat you that way, no matter what you said." She was furious. If only she could get a moment with that man, with a heavy vase in her hand or perhaps a stick, she'd make sure he never hurt another woman again. She'd have a word with Sally—surely the saloon owner could make sure that type of man never set foot in the place again.

Daisy looked up, and Hattie was dismayed to see the outline of the bruise around her eye darkening to a savage purple. "Oh, Hattie, me dear sweet girl…ye really are from another world, aren't ye? Don't ye know Sally's keepin' ye around just to get ye into the business? She says ye'd fetch a pretty penny. The only thing stoppin' her from makin' ye do it right now is the sheriff breathin' down her neck. Soon as he stops givin' ye his attention, ye'll end up like the rest of us. Mark my words."

Hattie recoiled in horror. "No, no…that's not right. Sally wouldn't do that. She cares about me—that's why she took me in. She told me so herself—said she couldn't bear to see me go hungry." She shook her head and stood to pace around the tiny room.

"How do ye think it all started with me?" Daisy's voice had dropped to a whisper. "I was just a girl when she took me in. Promised me the world. Told me how much she cared. Then when me other options were gone and I'd gotten used to livin' under a sturdy roof and eatin' three square meals a day, she told me if I didn't do as she asked, I'd have to leave. I'd be on me own, without a penny to me name or a friend in the world. Oh, she said she felt like a mother to me and wanted what was best for me, so couldn't I see to help her keep the place runnin', seein' as how she had bills to pay? It all began so simply—just one time, to help her keep the wolves at bay. And next thing I knew…" She wiped her eyes again.

Hattie rested her hands on her knees, her breath coming in great gasps and her head spinning. She thought she might throw up, though she hadn't eaten anything since the picnic the night before. Could Daisy be right? It sounded too horrible, but something about it rang true with things Sally had been saying since she arrived, about how much she cared and how she stood between Hattie and destitution.

"You just rest, Daisy dear. I'll hurry down to the kitchen and ask the cook for a poultice or some oil for your bruises and those awful cuts." She patted Daisy's arm, then dressed quickly. As she pinned the last hairpin, securing it in a chignon at the back of her head, she scurried from the room and down the long hall.

Hattie couldn't think about Daisy's words just then. She had to keep moving. There was nothing she could do about it right now except help her friend, so that's what she set her mind to. Then, when it was quiet later and she was alone with her thoughts, she'd think it all through. That would be the time to figure out a way forward.

Ed rubbed his wrist and grimaced. He'd taken a spill from his horse a week before when crossing a creek on the trail of what was now being called "the Miller Gang." His wrist had taken the bulk of his weight and was still tender. He turned his hand in a slow circle, working out the kinks, and fumed over his personal failure to track the men down.

He pushed his chair back from his desk and stood with a yawn. He wasn't the type of man who enjoyed sitting for long, but sometimes there was paperwork and he was the only one who could do it. Out of habit, he checked that the handgun on his left hip was loaded, flicking it open and spinning the chamber to count the bullets, then making sure the safety was still on. He closed and reholstered it, then repeated the procedure for the one on his opposite hip. "I'm just headin' out for a bit," he told Hans, who sat behind his desk with his feet propped on it.

Hans didn't move. His hat rested jauntily over his face, a light snore resounding from beneath it.

Lee glanced up from where he was stacking playing cards one on top of the other to build a paper fort. "Hokay, boss. See you later."

Ed shook his head. His deputies never did well when there wasn't enough to keep them occupied. Things had been quiet around town lately, and they'd run down every lead they had on the Miller Gang, to no avail. Since the stagecoach that had brought Hattie to town was robbed, nothing much had happened—just a few altercations involving drunken townsfolk, and boundary disputes between ranchers.

He marched out the door of the office and down the street. Thunderclouds gathered ominously overhead and he squinted up at the sky. He hoped it would rain— they sure needed it. Most likely the clouds would be blown off by the hot summer wind and they'd miss out again. This wasn't Virginia, where summer rain was normal—California got it in the winter, if it got it at all.

His mind strayed to thoughts of the church picnic, to Hattie Stout and the dance they'd shared. He hadn't been able to get her out of his mind, since that evening. Her touch was pure pleasure, her eyes doorways to Heaven. He'd tried to keep his distance, to convince himself she'd never look at him as anything other than the dusty sheriff of a dustier town that she'd once passed through. He knew better than to hope for more. And yet, hope was exactly the thing eating him up inside.

Just then he saw Hattie round the corner, headed in his direction. Her head was down and her bonnet flapped in the breeze. She held it in place with one hand and her skirts with the other as wind howled down the center of the street, buffeting her along with the rest of the pedestrians. A basket was slung over one arm, held snug against her side.

When she reached him, she looked up and her eyes sparked with recognition. "Sheriff, how nice to see you. Are you well?" Her voice was tense and her smile tight.

"Fine, thank you, Miss Stout. And you?" She looked beautiful, her hazel eyes wide and her skin glowing under the stormy light, the wind whipping her hair in every direction.

"Also fine, thank you." Her gaze dropped and she sighed.

"What is it?" he asked, stepping closer. He wished he could wrap his arms around her, but kept his distance.

"It's just…it's…well, I don't know what's to become

of me." She burst into tears and buried her face in her hands, sobbing dejectedly.

He frowned and rested a hand on her shoulder. She looked so sorrowful and alone, he could bear it no longer. He put his arms around her, and with a loud cry she fell against him, pressing her cheek to his shirt and clutching the fabric with both hands. "What is it? What's happened?" he whispered against her hair.

She didn't respond, just cried harder.

"Everythin's gonna be fine. It's all gonna work out, you'll see." He lifted a hand to stroke the back of her head.

"No, it's not. I don't have anywhere to go, no one who loves me. My parents sent me away, and now Sally…oh, I can't stay at the saloon. I just can't."

Ed took a slow breath. What had happened at the saloon to upset her so much? Admittedly, she had reason to be a little emotional. She was married to an outlaw, her entire family was still back east—she had reason to feel like she was all alone in the world, though as beautiful as she was it wasn't likely she'd stay that way for long. He should comfort her, say something to make her feel better. But what?

"Don't fret, Miss Stout—soon we'll have Jack Miller under lock and key, and you can be rid of him. Likely you'll meet a handsome cowboy to marry before too much time passes. There's plenty of good fellows 'round these parts, lookin' for a pretty young woman to grace their homes—oof!"

His eyebrows arched high in surprise as she pushed him violently away. "Well, thank you for that, I'm sure, Sheriff," she sniffed, pulling a handkerchief from her pocket to dry her nose and eyes.

He frowned. She seemed upset by what he'd said, though he couldn't for the life of him figure why. "I only meant that you're a mighty fine catch…"

She interrupted him with a frigid look that sent a chill down his spine. "As I said, thank you. Now if you don't mind, I'll be on my way. Sally sent me to buy more flour and I haven't much time." She lowered her head, put a hand on her bonnet and leaned into the wind as she continued down the street toward the mercantile.

Ed watched her go in confusion. It was obvious she'd been hurt by his words, but the why of it completely evaded him. He'd meant to compliment her, but instead seemed to have offended. Dagnabit, he never did know how to speak to women. He shook his head, shoved his hands deep into his pockets and continued on his way.

Chapter Six

Hattie plunged the stick into the butter churn, lifted it high and sent it deep into the milk once again. She sighed and ran the back of her wrist across her forehead, wiping away the line of perspiration. It was hard work, but she didn't mind. It had taken her a while to learn to do it well, but once she did, she liked the rhythm of it. And the mindlessness gave her a chance to think, which she certainly needed.

The church picnic had been such a wonderful evening. She'd left the lantern-dotted field with her heart soaring and her mind filled with images of herself and the sheriff dancing, his strong arms holding her steady. But even so, the idea of leaving Coloma always hovered in the back of her mind.

What about the sheriff?

And what about her husband?

She continued churning—the butter and her thoughts.

There was a knock on the kitchen door. Ed walked in and her heart leaped into her throat. "Sheriff! How nice to see you." She smoothed her hair back from her face as her pulse galloped. Just the sight of him made her knees go weak, especially when she recalled him holding her in the middle of the street when she'd broken down in tears.

Then she remembered what he'd said, and her stomach lurched—not to worry, she'd likely find some miner or farmer to marry her. He'd made it perfectly clear he didn't see himself doing it. Then why had he danced with her, held her so close?

"Good to see you also, Hattie. Do you…mind if I call you that?" He took off his hat and turned it in his weathered hands.

She nodded. "No, not at all."

"You can call me Ed. If you'd like."

"I would." She nodded approvingly, leaned the stick against the side of the churn and wiped her hands on her apron. "Tea?"

"Don't mind if I do." She poured a glass of iced tea and handed it to him, and he took it with a smile, his eyes sparkling. "Thank you." With a few swallows, he finished it, then set the empty glass down on the nearby table and wiped his mouth with his sleeve. "Delicious."

She licked her lips and clasped her hands in front of her skirts. "So what can I do for you… Ed?"

He scuffed the toe of his boot against the floor. "Hattie, I guess I was just wonderin'…well, if you'd let me court you? Generally speakin', I'd ask your pa about somethin' like that. But seeing as how he ain't here, I'm askin' you."

She raised an eyebrow. "Well, that is…um…yes, I would like that. Only…" She felt she should remind him that she was, technically, married. But she couldn't bring herself to say it. All she wanted was to walk out that door with Ed and never come back to the saloon.

If she sent him away...well, according to Daisy he was the only reason Sally didn't force her into a life of sin.

He grinned and slapped his hat back on. "That's wonderful. Well, how about a walk, then?"

"What? Now? I mean, I have to churn this butter, so..."

Mrs. Patterson the cook ambled into the kitchen and hung her bonnet on a peg by the door. She stopped when she saw the sheriff and wiped her hands on her apron. "Sheriff Milton, what a pleasant surprise."

"Hello, Mrs. Patterson. You're looking mighty handsome today. Did you change your hair?"

Hattie tipped her head to one side—he certainly could be charming when he felt the need.

Mrs. Patterson's eyelids fluttered. "You honey-tongued devil, you," she stammered, patting her wispy blonde-gray locks.

"I was just about to take Hattie for a walk. You don't mind, do you?"

Mrs. Patterson shook her head quickly. "Of course not. You young folk go outside and enjoy the sunshine. I'll finish up with the butter."

Hattie didn't wait around for the old woman to change her mind. She tugged off her apron and hurried from the room with the sheriff close behind. "Thank you, Mrs. Patterson," she called over her shoulder, and heard Ed chuckle softly behind her.

Outside, he offered her his arm and she rested her hand on his shirt sleeve with a flush in her cheeks. He was so tall, and she could feel his strength as she brushed up against him. She glanced up at him with a tentative smile and he returned it with a wink that made her heart melt.

They walked in silence down the street until they came to the outskirts of town. She could see the mines stretching off to the north. A road wound westward, and they followed it through rolling hills lined with oaks and bushes. A jackrabbit loped along a ridge, stopping to look back at them with wary curiosity.

Hattie took a long slow breath of country air. It felt good to escape the bustle of the dusty town for a little while. She didn't realize until that moment how much she'd needed this—she'd felt as though she could barely breathe sometimes. A smile drifted across her face.

Ed saw it and patted her hand where it rested on his arm. "I know things have been difficult for you. But, if there's anythin' I can do to help you...you only have to ask."

Her eyes closed for a moment and she sighed. "Thank you, Ed. I appreciate it."

"Can I ask you something?"

"Of course." She squinted into the morning sunlight as it beat down on their heads.

"Your folks really couldn't find anything for you other than sending you west?"

"Apparently not." She caught his eye with a half-smile and a long sigh. "So here I am."

He stopped and turned to face her, laying his hands softly on her shoulders. "Yes, here you are. But will you stay?"

"Stay in Coloma?" Her thoughts swirled. Only hours earlier she'd have answered him vehemently, with a re-sounding "No." But now she wavered. "I don't know..." She pined for home, but Ed's touch made her tremble and his kindnesses to her over the previous weeks had fortified her with a strength she never realized she had. Still, with all the instability of her sham of a marriage and her employment at a place one step shy of a brothel…was he reason enough to stay?

A second of stillness. Then he pulled her to him, crushing her mouth with his. She gasped. She'd never kissed a man like that before. Never felt that tug, that spark of attraction that might tempt her to step over the bounds of propriety, not even when she was engaged. But now, in the blinding California sunshine, worlds away from the drawing rooms and dance floors of New York City, she let go of her fears, her turmoil and her worries for a moment in time. A single perfect moment.

Even as her heart beat against his ribcage, the doubts returned with a vengeance. What was she doing? She shouldn't be kissing the sheriff. For one, she was married. And secondly, she had to get home to New York— as much as he made her feel things she'd never felt before, she couldn't lose her focus or she'd end up destitute and alone in the California wilderness. She put her hands against his chest and pushed him away.

His eyes blinked open, his gaze locked with hers and his hands clenched at his sides. "What's wrong, Hattie?"

She covered her mouth and stifled a sob. "I'm sorry, Ed. You know I'm married. Yes, my husband is an outlaw and a scoundrel, but it doesn't change that. And I know you won't likely understand this, but I have to get home, back to my family. The saloon is not where I want to spend my days. There's nothing for me there. I'm saving my pennies, then catching the train back east…" She paused when she saw the look in his eyes.

He turned away and strode further down the trail away from town. Stopping suddenly, he spoke without facing her. "Is there anything I can say to change your mind?"

She shook her head. "I don't know what you could say that would make any difference. Things are the way they are."

He put his hands on his hips. "Well, I guess that's it, then."

"Hattie!" called Daisy, stamping her foot outside their bedroom door.

Hattie fastened the last pin in her hat and hurried outside. "Coming!"

"That's what you've been saying the past half-hour," complained Daisy.

They hurried along the dark, dusty hallway, down the stairs and through the saloon. Sally stood behind the bar and called out to them as they passed through the door. "Don't be late comin' back, ya hear?"

Daisy giggled and took hold of Hattie's arm once they were outside. "I'm so glad to be free!" she cried, throwing her head back and letting the sun warm her face.

Hattie smiled. "It does feel good."

"And we're going to a play."

"Well, to be fair, it's not Broadway…but I'm just as excited as you are." Hattie took a long, deep breath and smiled at the passersby as they bustled through town. They'd miss the opening curtain if they didn't hurry—Sally hadn't let them finish work early as they'd asked to.

Also, Hattie hadn't been able to decide on the right hairstyle. She knew it likely didn't matter, since no one in Coloma knew the first thing about the latest fashions. But she hadn't seen Ed since that fateful kiss. Yes, she'd pushed him away, but the thought of seeing him again made her heart pound and her palms grow damp.

They hurried into the church hall, and Hattie grimaced to see every pew already full. The audience was quiet too, which meant the show was about to start. She and Daisy slid into chairs in the back of the room, and she craned her neck to see over the heads between her and the temporary stage that had been erected at the front.

"What's the play called?" asked Daisy, foraging through her reticule with a frown.

Hattie glanced at the silent audience around them. A few shot Daisy irritated looks. "Um... The Lights O' London," she whispered in Daisy's ear, trying hard not to cause a disturbance.

"Do we know anyone in the play?" asked Daisy loudly, pulling two long candy canes from her reticule. She handed one to Hattie with a grin and stuck the other in her mouth, sucking hard. Someone told her to shush, but she just rolled her eyes.

Hattie sighed and placed the candy in her lap. "I'm not sure," she whispered. "I believe Deputy Perez might be playing Clifford."

Just then, the music began and actors filed onto the stage. Hattie gasped—there was Ed! He was dressed in a black suit with a matching top hat, and when he doffed his hat she could see that his hair was neatly combed. She almost couldn't recognize him. He looked so dapper and handsome, his beard trimmed and his broad chest and narrow hips well suited to the tailored clothing.

"Oh look, it's Ed!" declared Daisy, taking the candy

from her mouth long enough to disrupt everyone around her, then shoving it back in to slurp noisily.

"Shhh…" Hattie whispered, covering her eyes. Daisy would get them thrown out of a Coloma community production before it was over, something she never would have thought likely.

Daisy simply smiled, her eyes sparkling with mischief. But she didn't cause further trouble.

The play proceeded reasonably smoothly, apart from two incidents. In the first, a small boy in the play, wearing a pair of pants that were much too large, had his suspenders give way, displaying his tattered undergarments to the audience. He burst into tears, stormed from the stage and refused to return even though he played a major part. This gave the rest of the performance a disjointed air, as the other actors on stage tried to fill in his lines as best they could. When it happened, Daisy convulsed in fits of mercifully quiet laughter.

Then, near the dramatic end of the play, Ed misstepped and fell off the stage, landing in Mrs. Sandringham's lap. The old woman had just fallen asleep, and the shock of it almost gave her a heart attack. She picked up her walking cane and whacked Ed over the head and shoulders with it repeatedly until he climbed back up, clutching his wounded head with both hands. By this time, Daisy and Hattie were both doubled over with laughter, but so was most of the audience, so no one minded.

The actors did a fine job of picking things up where they'd left off and finishing the performance. Then the thespians (absent the one boy and his drawers) linked hands across the small stage and bowed to thunderous applause.

Daisy and Hattie wandered from the building, clutching at each other for support as they continued to laugh. "Oh, that was the best show I've ever seen," cried Daisy, dabbing at fresh tears with a clean handkerchief.

Hattie puffed hard, trying desperately to compose herself. "I can't…breathe…" she laughed. "Did you see Ed's face? Oh, it was priceless."

"I'm glad you enjoyed it."

Hattie spun around, eyes wide, to find Ed behind them. "Ed, you were wonderful. Well done." She smiled widely and quickly dried the tears from her cheeks with her gloves.

He raised an eyebrow. "Thank you. Though I could hear the two of you cacklin' all the way through."

Hattie held her breath, all temptation to giggle gone. "I'm sorry. Were you hurt?"

"Don't pretend concern now." Ed kept a stone face for another moment, then burst into laughter. "I'm just teasin'. It really was a hoot. I'm just glad old Mrs. Sandringham didn't bust my head with her cane." The three of them laughed together, Hattie with some relief. Then Ed offered Hattie one arm and Daisy the other. "Let's get somethin' to eat."

They walked to where people had set up tables covered in goodies and picnic rugs on the ground. Picnickers were scattered around, holding plates in their hands, laughing and chatting. "Will ye look at all this food!" exclaimed Daisy. She let go of Ed's arm and hurried over to a table to find a plate.

"You really were very good," said Hattie, her cheeks burning.

Ed's eyes sparked with humor. "Yes, well…it must have been entertaining."

"It was," she gushed, then laughed again. "Though I'm not sure Broadway will be calling."

He tipped his hat back. "Not likely. Just as well I have a job already, I suppose."

"Are you hungry?" she asked.

"Famished."

They fixed themselves two plates of bread rolls, salt pork, beans, turkey and dressing, then sat on a nearby unoccupied picnic rug. As they ate, Ed shared more about his family back in Virginia, how he'd always wanted to be a teacher, but when he'd traveled west he couldn't seem to stop moving. He loved the adventure of it and always wondered what he might find further on. He'd kept going until he reached the Pacific coast, then turned back and settled in Coloma.

"They needed a sheriff then, not a teacher, so that's what I became. I wasn't sure I'd like it, but it's turned out fine. I can help people just as much as if I was a teacher. And the town's become home to me."

Hattie could testify to that. While they sat there, everyone who walked by greeted Ed with a smile and asked him how he was doing. For the most part, people seemed to view him with great esteem and affection, and she admired him all the more because of it.

When he finally took her home after the celebration, he did so like a perfect gentleman. She was disappointed he didn't try to kiss her. Her lips tingled as her eyes met his. But it was her own fault for pushing him away the last time. He didn't know where he stood with her because she wasn't sure either. In her head she knew she shouldn't start anything with a man she'd likely never see again once she left Coloma.

But Hattie couldn't help wishing for one more kiss; to have Ed hold her in his arms and never let go.

Chapter Seven

Hattie flapped the wet shirt in the air in an effort to smooth out the wrinkles, then hung it over the line of string that ran between two sticks set in the ground. Her bonnet slipping over her eyes, she tugged a peg from between her teeth and clamped it on the shirt to hold it in place.

Daisy pegged a petticoat to the line beside her and laughed. "Hain't ye ever done this before? That shirt looks like a blind man threw it at the line."

Hattie rolled her eyes and tossed a wet pair of drawers at Daisy, hitting her in the face. She peeled them off with a guffaw and pegged them to the line.

Still melancholy over the way things ended with Ed after the play, Hattie sighed and let her shoulders slump while she worked.

"What's wrong with ye, princess?" asked Daisy, taking a huge bite of a roll she pulled from her apron pocket. She chewed slowly, her narrowed eyes fixed on Hattie.

"If I was to go back east, would you come with me?" blurted Hattie.

Daisy's eyes went wide. "What?"

"I want you to come with me." Hattie pegged another shirt to the line, then smoothed a strand of hair from her eyes.

Daisy laughed, but this time the sound was strained. "What would I do, sleep on the settee in the drawing room? I'm sure your Pa would love ye bringin' a girl like me home."

"I don't know—I just can't leave you here, not with things the way they are. And I'm leaving as soon as I can."

"What about the sheriff?"

Tears pricked Hattie's eyes, but she brushed them away with a swipe of her hand. "It's no use. I'm married, and he's…well, he's here. And I don't want to be—here, that is." The words fell awkwardly from her mouth.

There was a shout and Hattie spun around to see a wagon trundling by on the road into town, packed to the brim with children of all ages. The noise seemed to have come from a scuffle between several of them. Two sleek bay horses trotted in the traces, and she could see the sheriff's black hat behind them. He hunched over the reins, facing forward and ignoring the commotion in the wagon bed. "What's going on there?" she asked.

Daisy stepped forward to stand beside her, still chewing on the bread. "What, the wagon? Looks like another bunch of the sheriff's orphans." Her lips smacking, she took another large bite.

Hattie eyed her in confusion. "He has orphans?"

Daisy grinned. "He collects 'em from all 'round the county, brings 'em back and finds families to take 'em in. Any left, he sends on to San Francisco to the orphan asylum. A lot of 'em lost their families on the drive west, others when they arrived. Either way, they're on their own. Sheriff Milton likes to find them somewhere to go."

Hattie's eyes widened. This was a side to Ed she hadn't seen before. He was rugged and strong and she'd witnessed how people around town respected him, but ferrying a wagonful of rowdy orphans into town? He was full of surprises. "Where do they stay until he can find them a family?"

"I think the sheriff's office. He usually collects 'em when the jail cells are empty and things are quiet. Feeds 'em all out of his own pocket, he does. He's a good man, our sheriff."

Hattie's throat ached. She'd never met a man like Ed Milton before. Back in New York, every man she knew was only interested in money, power and status. In her circle of acquaintances, it would have been unheard of for a man to take his own time and money, gather orphans together and feed them.

She smoothed her hair out of her eyes as the wagon disappeared behind the tall facade of the mercantile, headed for the sheriff's office. He'd make someone a fine husband and a good father to his children one day, that much was clear. She'd misjudged him so many times, and hadn't truly given him a chance.

"What're ye thinkin' about so serious over there?" asked Daisy with a smirk as she tucked the now-empty clothes basket beneath her arm.

Hattie picked up her own basket and sighed. "Just wishing I'd had the good sense not to marry that cad Jack Miller. Now I'm tied to him and…oh, why is everything always so complicated?"

The two women walked toward the back door of the saloon, side by side. "Ye know," began Daisy, shifting the basket onto her other hip. "Old Man Hurley was in yesterday, and I told him about your predicament."

"You mean the retired lawyer from Boston?"

"Aye, that's the one. Well, he said since ye never really were with your husband—ye know, as man and wife—ye could get this thing called an annulment. Like ye were never actually married. They could do it down at the courthouse."

Hattie pulled the door open, following Daisy into the steamy kitchen as her stomach churned. "Really? Is that possible?"

"He seemed to think it was. And it can't hurt to find out, can it?"

Hattie's head spun. Could it be so easy? She'd go to the courthouse as soon as possible to ask about it. Perhaps she'd soon only remember all that had happened as if it were a bad dream, to be left in the past.

She hurried into the laundry room and set the empty basket on the floor. Too bad she had so much work to do before lunch, or she'd go right now. Never mind— tomorrow she'd have a chance. Mrs. Patterson always sent her to the mercantile on Tuesdays with a list of groceries—she'd stop by the courthouse then.

Hans and Lee were backed against the front wall of the sheriff's office, their wide eyes drifting over a sea of dirty faces. Ed grinned. His deputies had never gotten used to him gathering orphans when the jail cells were empty and letting them stay there until he could place them with families.

Hans went out the front door and lit up his pipe.

Lee squatted beside a small boy struggling to bite off
a piece of the bread Ed had given him. He smiled and
took out his pocket knife to cut the bread into pieces
for him. At first the boy looked terrified by the knife,
but soon Lee had him smiling and even offered him
the knife to take a look, showing him how to hold it
carefully. The boy turned it over with eyes as round
as saucers as he chewed on the bread.

Ed handed out the last piece of bread to the tallest
girl in the group. She took it with a grateful smile and
dip of the head. His heart went out to the poor mites.
They'd lost everything. Most of them had come west
with their folks, some with brothers and sisters, and
now they were on their own. Some still had their siblings, but others had no one. And for people out here,
life was a constant struggle, so taking in another mouth
to feed wasn't a priority. Without his help, most of
them would likely starve or be taken by wild animals.

Ed stepped carefully between the rows of warm
bodies as he made his way to the door. "Hey, Lee, I'm
headin' out for a bit. Can you watch 'em for me?"

Lee stood up, looking panicked. "What? Going
where?"

"Just up to the saloon for a bit. You'll be great with
'em." Ed chuckled and put his hat on as he stood in the
doorway surveying the packed room.

"What do I do with all these *niños*?" asked Lee. The
swarthy deputy was surrounded by children, their dirt-
streaked faces turned up to him like flowers drawn to
the warmth of the sun.

"Play a game or somethin'," said Ed. "Little'uns love
games." He turned and set off down the street, ignoring Lee's calls after him. It'd be good for his deputy

to spend some time with the children. He was always saying he wished he could find a woman, settle down and have a family—this was his chance to get a taste of it. Of course, he might well change his tune after an hour or so. Ed chuckled to himself at the thought of it.

He entered the saloon hoping to see Hattie, though after the way she'd left things between them, he wasn't entirely certain she'd want to see him. He'd been determined to keep his distance—after all, when he'd kissed her, she'd pushed him away. But then he'd seen her at the play, and he could've sworn there was a spark of attraction between them. And after bringing the children back to town, all he wanted to do was see her. He couldn't get his mind to focus on anything else. He leaned against the bar, ordered a finger of whiskey from Sally, tipped his hat back and waited.

It wasn't long before she shuffled in with a mop and bucket. The handle of the mop kept knocking her in the head as she pushed the bucket full of sudsy water forward with her feet. He covered his mouth with his hand, coughing to mask his mirth.

There was something so intriguing, innocent and delightful about Hattie Stout. He'd never met a woman who made him feel this way before. She could be infuriating, yet gentle as a lamb. He never knew what she'd say or do from one moment to the next. Probably because he'd never met a debutante from New York City before—she certainly stood out like a sore thumb in this worn-out mining town.

He downed the last of the whiskey, wiped his mouth on his sleeve, stood and headed toward her. "Hattie…" He didn't know what to say next.

She turned to him with a warm smile that lit up her

sparkling hazel eyes. "Ed! How nice to see you. I was wondering when you'd stop by."

He paused and scratched the side of his beard with his fingertips. "Uh…yeah. Well, I've been busy."

Her tinkling laugh turned his legs to jelly. "So I hear. What a wonderful thing you're doing, taking care of those children. There aren't many who would, that's for sure." As she spoke, she rested her hand on his forearm and sent a spark of heat running through his body.

"Yes, well… I think it's the least I can do. I hate to think of them out there all alone in the wild."

He stared down at her hand. Long, delicate fingers resting on his shirt sleeve. "Would you like to take a walk?"

She nodded and set the mop and bucket behind the bar, then took his arm and walked out to the street with him. "I can't be long. Sally wants me to mop the floor until it 'dang shines,' her words. Though I don't know if that floor could ever shine again, even if I took a scrub brush to it on my knees. But as Daisy says, what Sally wants, Sally gets."

He set his hand on hers and relished the feel of her soft skin beneath his palm. He drank in her beauty and the blush of her cheeks. "You seem in a fine mood."

"I am."

He raised an eyebrow as they strolled down the street. "Any hints as to why?"

"I don't want to say too much just yet, since I'm not certain…but I see a light at the end of the dark tunnel I've been journeying through. I promise, I'll tell you all about it very soon."

He smiled. "Well then, I'll hold you to it."

"You may indeed." Her eyes twinkled and she sighed. "Things are starting to look brighter."

What was she referring to? It was possible she'd saved enough for her fare back to New York. Or maybe it was something else. If only she'd tell him—he could hardly bear the wait. "When do you think you'll be ready to share your news?"

"Oh, in a few days, I believe."

"So if I call on you again in three days…"

"Why three days?" She pursed her lips.

"I'm aimin' to get the orphans settled by then."

She smiled. "That sounds perfect."

They turned around and headed back to the saloon. The afternoon sun burned bright overhead, and Ed could feel it scorching his black hat, making his head sweat. A trickle of damp meandered down his back and he stopped at the entrance to the saloon. "I'll see you in three days, then," he said, cupping her hand between his.

Her cheeks flamed brighter. "Yes, until then," she replied, her voice almost a whisper.

He doffed his hat, leaned over her, her lips enticing him, drawing him in. She closed her eyes and lifted her chin. When their lips met, he knew he wanted to spend the rest of his days with her wrapped in his arms.

She stepped back, her eyes flicking open, and grinned. "Goodbye, Ed."

As he strode back to the office, his smile broadened until it almost split his face in two. It was a fine day. A very fine day indeed.

Chapter Eight

Hattie ran her brush through her hair which snapped and sparked beneath her hand. She set the brush on the dressing table and gazed at her reflection in the looking glass, the flame of the candle on the table beside her flickering. She picked up the candle holder and carried it to her bedside table.

It had been a long day—she'd scrubbed, scoured, washed and fetched until she was bone-tired. Sally was occasionally motivated to get the saloon in shape, and today had been one of those days. The rest of the time she seemed not to care whether it slid into a pit of filth. But today she'd wanted everything to sparkle and Hattie was the one to do it. She sighed and sat down on the bed with relief.

Just then, she heard a muffled shout, followed by a loud crash and a scream. She jumped up and ran to the door, flinging it open and looking up and down the long dark hallway. She wished Coloma had electric lights like more developed cities around the country. Edison's light bulb had amazed her the first time she saw one, and had made everyone's lives so much more civilized. But Coloma wasn't New York City.

She ran back to get the candle, guarding the flame with her hand as she rushed out again and down the hall. The awful noise continued, beckoning her onward. When it stopped, she halted her headlong pace to listen intently. She heard a noise through a nearby closed door—a sobbing that tore at her heart.

She knocked on the door. When there was no response, she turned the handle and pushed it open. "Hello? It's Hattie, I just wanted to check on you, make sure you're all right. Hello?" The sobbing was louder now. Then she saw a man standing by a mussed bed, buckling a holster around his narrow hips, and gasped. "Hans?"

Deputy Hans Bergman came toward her, his badge flashing in the light from the lantern that hung by the door. He stood so close that she could smell the tobacco and whiskey on his breath, and sneered, revealing stained teeth. "Hullo, Hattie." His voice was a growl, like gravel beneath the wheel of a wagon.

She reeled back, her hand covering her mouth. "Hans, what in Heaven's name are you up to? I'll speak to Ed about you…"

"I think it best ya mind yer own business, else I can't be sure I can protect you, if ya know what I'm gettin' at." He glowered and raised a hand as though to hit her, lowered it to his side and glanced over his shoulder toward the corner of the room. Then he dashed past her out the door and down the stairs to the saloon.

Hattie leaned back against the open door with a sigh of relief. Then she ventured into the corner of the room where the sobbing came from, and all relief fled.

"Daisy!" She ran to her friend's side and knelt beside her, setting the candle on the floor. Already she could see the bruises emerging on Daisy's pale cheeks and around her left eye. Her arms were reddened with ugly welts in the shape of long fingers and her nightgown was torn and bunched up around her waist. "Oh no! Are you all right, my dear Daisy?"

Daisy couldn't speak, only weep and whimper.

Hattie's throat closed around a lump as her eyes flooded with tears. She helped her friend to her feet with a gentle hand beneath her elbow. "Come on, dear, back to our room."

Daisy hobbled with Hattie's help back to their bedroom. Hattie helped her into bed, filled the washbowl from the jug of water and used a washcloth to dab at Daisy's bruises. "I'm sorry it's cold," she murmured, smoothing Daisy's hair back.

Daisy hiccupped softly, her cheeks streaked with tears.

Hattie's sorrow was quickly replaced with burning anger. "You can't keep doing this, Daisy! It's not right. There has to be another way." She choked back a sob of her own and set the washcloth back in the bowl.

Daisy met her gaze with reddened eyes. "What else can I do? I ain't got a family. I ain't got a place to go. This is it for me." She buried her face in her hands and burst into fresh tears.

Hattie sighed deeply. She didn't know what to say. If only she had money, she'd get Daisy far away from the Roan Horse. But she couldn't even rescue herself. "Well, I'm going to talk with Sally tomorrow. She must not be aware that this is going on. Maybe she'll let you do something else—you could work in the kitchen with me, couldn't you?" That was it—she just knew Sally would see reason.

Daisy touched Hattie's arm with a wry smile. "Ye're a sweet thing. But it won't work—Sally don't care. I know you think she does, but she don't. I'm grateful to you for thinkin' of it though."

Hattie watched Sally out of the corner of her eye as she swept out the office. The proprietress of the Roan Horse was counting the cash from the cashbox, and Hattie never knew what kind of mood the woman would be in after she was done. It all depended on the take. When it wasn't high enough for her liking, the employees would steer clear of her for hours, tiptoeing around the place, hoping desperately not to be the object of her wrath.

And someone always was, depending on who irritated her first. Last month it had been Nicky, the young boy who helped in the stables. He'd come into the kitchen for an apple right as Sally stormed through. Thankfully, Hattie hadn't yet had the misfortune to be in her way at those times.

The cashbox lid fell shut, Sally smiled and caught Hattie's eye, her own eyes twinkling. "Hattie, my dear, have you finished with the dusting?"

Hattie set the broom against the wall with a nod and scurried to Sally's side, smiling warmly. "Yes, Sally, and I just finished the sweeping."

"Good girl," said Sally, patting her arm.

"Sally, there's something I wanted to discuss with you."

Sally had already turned away—she'd picked up the

cashbox and was headed for the wall safe in her office. Her face was a study in concentration. "Hmmm…"

"I don't know if you've seen Daisy today, but she was beaten up pretty bad by Hans Bergman last night."

Sally glanced at her, her smile dissipating. "That so?"

"Yes, and I just think she really shouldn't work… that way…any longer. It's not safe for her. I was thinking maybe she could work in the kitchen. Mrs. Patterson is always so busy, she could do with the help, and…"

Sally stepped closer and smiled sweetly, but her eyes were cold. "Yes, my dear, I hear you—you're worried 'bout your friend and that's admirable. But I need Daisy to continue doin' what she's doin'. She helps keep this place afloat. Without her and the other girls, we wouldn't have a roof over our heads for long. In fact, since you raised the subject, I've been meanin' to talk to you 'bout your place here."

Hattie blinked and swallowed hard. She didn't like the look in Sally's eyes and braced for the words that came next.

"It's time for you to take on more responsibility for our little family here. Daisy and the girls need help. There's an abundance of work, and not many to do it. And I think yer just the woman for the job."

"Do you mean to say you expect me to become a sporting woman as well?" Hattie hissed, her hands on her hips.

"I do indeed," Sally snarled, all pretense at friendliness gone. "Did you think ya could mooch off me forever, girl?"

"I've hardly been mooching…"

Sally poked Hattie's shoulder, making her step back. "It's high time for you to do yer duty. And if you won't, ya can hit the street—and I mean tomorrow, girl. So you best have a think 'bout it if you know what's good for ya. Let me know what you decide." She smiled wickedly, then went off to stow the money box in the safe.

Hattie stumbled away, tears blurring her vision. What could she do? She had nowhere to go and hadn't saved enough money for train fare back east yet. If she didn't do as Sally said, she'd be homeless in a day. She covered her mouth to muffle her sobs and ran up the stairs as fast as she could, throwing herself down on the bed and covered her head with her pillow before letting the tears fall.

Ed slapped the traces along the backs of the bay horses and whistled as they plodded along. Behind him in the wagon bed, the remaining children laughed and chattered.

He glanced over his shoulder at them and smiled. They'd come out of their shells so much the past two days. When he'd first collected them, they'd been wary and silent, but now they were full of life. He'd even seen them running and playing when they'd stopped at the last two ranches. Just one child, a girl of about four, sat silently and stared at the horizon. Every attempt he'd made to engage her in conversation had come to naught, but he was determined to get her talking before the journey was over.

So far, he'd managed to place five children in homes around Coloma. There were six more to go, and he was determined to do it in the next twenty-four hours, so he could go home and call on Hattie. He missed her more than he'd expected—just the thought of her set his heart racing and brought a smile to his face.

He mulled over the letter he'd received from his sister Rosalind back in Virginia. He'd been grateful to finally hear of her baby's arrival—another girl to add to the family tree. A wave of homesickness washed over him. He couldn't meet his niece, but at least he could help these children who had no one but him to care for them.

Ed pulled the horses to a halt outside a small, sturdy farmhouse. A vegetable garden, bigger than the house itself, filled the space between it and an even bigger barn. A man behind a plow being pulled by a team of oxen waved from the field beyond. He returned the wave and stepped down from the wagon. The children piled out behind him and chattered with excitement, having become accustomed to the process. Each of them wondered out loud who would be chosen, if any, to stay with this family.

Ed strode toward the house as a woman bustled outside, a baby in her arms. She smiled and met Ed with an outstretched hand. "Sheriff Milton, so good to see you," she murmured, glancing over his shoulder at the children behind him, their round eyes full of eagerness.

He shook her hand and took off his hat "Mrs. Brown, it's been too long. Are you well? I see you have a new addition to the family."

She laughed. "Yes, I do. Ann's a good eater and a fine sleeper, so I'm doing as well as you'd expect given there are eight more beside her."

The sheriff arched an eyebrow. "It's hard to believe when you don't look a day over twenty, Mrs. Brown."

She giggled and brushed her flyaway hair back with her free hand. "You're always the charmer, Sheriff. What brings you out our way?"

"Well, I've got another wagonload of orphans, as you can see. Just wonderin' if you need any help 'round the farm. Some of 'em are strong and willing to work hard."

She frowned. "I don't know, Sheriff. We've got so many mouths to feed already…" Again her eyes drifted past his shoulder, settling on the small silent girl still sitting in the wagon. She wandered over to the girl and stood in front of her, smiling warmly. "But, one thing I don't have is a sister for this little 'un. Eight boys and only one girl. Mr. Brown's happy, of course—he's got help in the field. But my little Ann could do with a sister and I'm not likely to have more, according to the doc." She lifted a hand to caress the girl's cheek. "What's your name, little one?"

The girl's large green eyes met Mrs. Brown's and she took a quick breath. "Emma," she whispered, so quietly that Ed had to strain to hear it.

"Well, Emma, you're a right pretty thing, you are."

She turned back to face Ed, shifting the baby to her other arm with a sigh. "I'll have to speak with Mr. Brown, but I think we might have space for the girl."

Ed grinned. "That sounds mighty fine, Mrs. Brown."

Chapter Nine

The wind yowled through the streets of Coloma, whipping debris into the air. Trees bent low, their branches shivering and people leaned forward to press their way through it.

Hattie closed her eyes and wiped them in an attempt to clear the dust—and the tears. Where was Ed? He'd promised to be back by now, and Sally had only given her until the end of the day to move her things out of the saloon or become a…a…it didn't even bear thinking about. She wrapped her arms around herself as she glanced skyward, and swallowed hard at the angry black clouds swirling overhead. It wouldn't be long until the storm hit.

She was on her way to the sheriff's office to find Ed. If he'd returned from his quest of finding homes for all the orphans, he should be there. She hadn't seen Hans since the incident with Daisy. When she'd asked around town about him, no one had seen him, and she'd been met with various questioning looks and shakes of the head. He must have assumed she'd tell Ed what she saw and fled.

She finally reached the office, sighing with relief to be out of the gale. Lee sat behind Ed's desk, his feet resting on top, twirling his pistol around one finger. He leaped to his feet and reholstered his gun. "Sorry, *Señorita* Stout. Um… I was just…"

"Never mind that, Lee. Where is Ed? Is he back yet?" She glanced hopefully around the office, then frowned when she found the deputy was its only occupant.

"No, *señorita*, I have not seen him yet, but he should be back soon. And Hans has not come in today or yesterday—he was supposed to be here with me while Sheriff Milton is away." He scratched his head and shuffled his feet awkwardly.

Hattie exhaled slowly. "I saw him two days ago, but not since. You know, he beat up Daisy down at the Roan Horse pretty badly. So he might be in hiding, since he knows how fond Ed is of Daisy."

Lee's frown was deep. "He hit *Señorita* Sweeney? Ohhh, I am sure the sheriff will not like that. *I* do not like that."

Hattie braced herself to go outside and face the approaching storm again. "Well, please do let me know when Ed gets back. I really need to see him as soon as possible." Lee assured her that he would.

As she left, she shivered at the voluminous clouds marked by flashes of jagged lightning that lit up the darkened afternoon sky. She ducked her head and pulled her scarf up over her hair to scurry back toward the saloon. There was nothing for it. She'd have to pack her bags and spend the first night on her own in the worst storm she'd seen since she arrived in town. Her throat constricted and she shut her eyes for a moment.

But she opened them again filled with resolve. Never mind, she'd survive. But she certainly wouldn't do what Sally demanded of her. She would never be so desperate that she'd give up her honor for a roof over her head.

The saloon came into view just as the first fat raindrop landed on her cheek. She put one hand on top of her bonnet, gathered her skirts with the other and ran the rest of the way. A crash of thunder split the air around her and she jolted at the sound, her eyes widening in fright.

She stopped and looked back at the town. Buggies hurried down the street, drivers bringing whips down on the backs of galloping horses. Miners trotted quickly along covered sidewalks. A single child crossed the street in a rush of flying arms and legs, disappearing into one of the storefronts.

On a whim, she raised her face skyward to the rain. It felt so good to allow the dust and grime of the day to be washed away by those cool, heavy drops. She smiled and closed her eyes as the refreshing shower ran down her cheeks. Only when she felt it begin to soak through her bonnet did she turned to head inside.

But just as she did, two strong arms closed around her and a grimy hand clamped over her open mouth. She screamed into the palm of the man's hand, then her eyes found his face. No!

Jack Miller leaned close and whispered against her hair. "Hello, darlin'. Good to see ya again." He threw her onto the back of a pale horse, leaped up behind her and galloped away from the saloon and town as fast as the creature's legs would carry them.

She writhed and screamed, but the noise of the

storm drowned out her cries and carried them away on the wind. With everyone locked safely away inside their homes and stores, no one saw her skirts swirling and arms flailing as she rode by.

Jack's strong arms held her in place, tight and hard, while he urged his mount onward. They passed through the valley and away from the river, winding deeper between rolling hillsides following the path of a narrow creek, dogwood and lilac bushes squatting along its shores. After two hours he let his mount slow to a walk, then stop at the creek's edge to drink. The animal, sides heaving, lowered its head and took great gulps of the fresh, clear water.

Hattie struggled again, furiously trying to break his hold. He just chuckled and held her tighter as she screamed in frustration.

Two other men pulled their horses up behind them and waded the animals into the shallows to drink. They greeted Jack with a nod and grin, each pulling their own flask from a saddlebag to drink. One wore a neckerchief pulled up high on his face; the other had a wild-looking red beard which reached almost to his belt.

Jack tapped her on the shoulder and passed her a canteen. She took it and drank gratefully. She was exhausted, having never spent much time on a horse's back—certainly not in the months since arriving in Coloma. Her entire body groaned at every move she made, and she swallowed the water down quickly until her gut sloshed with it.

Jack climbed down, waded into the creek and refilled his canteen, satiating his own thirst as the water creeped up his pants legs. She took a long slow breath. What to do now? She wasn't sure what Jack was plan-

ning, but it didn't seem as though he had any intention
of returning her to town. She lifted her leg over the
saddle to lower herself onto the creek bank.

Jack slapped her on the rear with a growl. "No, ya
don't. Back up ya go—we ain't done ridin' yet."

With a grimace, she righted herself and waited while
he climbed back into place. The three outlaws moved
off together, climbing ever higher up a long hill covered in oaks and alders, their green foliage cloaking
the hillside and hiding the ground from view.

"Where are we going?" she asked, not for the first
time. Her earlier requests had been ignored, but perhaps now that their pace had slowed she'd have better luck.

Jack grunted and tightened his hold on her. "Never
you mind. Yer my wife, you go where I do. And while
we're on the subject, I really didn't 'preciate you turnin'
me in to the sheriff on our wedding day. Not real romantic of ya, I reckon."

She raised an eyebrow. "Your wife?"

"That's what you are, ain'tcha?"

She exhaled slowly. "Not for long. I've already ap-
plied at the courthouse to have our marriage annulled.
So I suppose officially I'm still your wife, but as soon
as the paperwork is processed, I won't be any longer."

"I don't know what that all means," he snarled. "All
I know is we said vows in front of the old fellow at the
courthouse and we're hitched. That's good enough for
me."

She turned her head and shifted in her seat to see his
face. "Why do you want to be married at all? You're
an outlaw, always on the run. I'd just slow you down."

His empty eyes fixed on hers as he sneered at her,

but the man with the red beard spoke before he could. "That's a good question," he said mockingly, his eyes narrowed at Jack.

Jack shifted in the saddle. "We're done with this place—we're headin' south to Mexico. And I liked the look of ya that first day I saw ya at the Roan Horse. I think ya'll make me a fine wife."

The other man coughed and wheeled his horse away from them. "She'll only make trouble for us, Jack," he called over his shoulder. "I've said it before and I'll say it again—not that you listen."

She frowned. It seemed not everyone was thrilled with Jack's idea to kidnap her. But was there enough of a schism between the men to give her an opportunity for escape?

As they drew closer to the crest of the hill, the branches overhead thinned. They came upon a quaint cabin, and the three men pulled their horses up short and led them into a small yard fenced in with rough-hewn logs. Jack helped Hattie to the ground before the men removed saddles and bridles and rubbed each animal down carefully, leaving her standing there. Only when the others began to feed and water their mounts did Jack lead her into the cabin.

She marveled at how well the cabin faded into the forest, as if it had just grown there. Anyone who didn't know exactly where to find it would likely ride right by without an inkling it was there.

Once she stepped inside, Hattie could smell the tobacco, wood smoke and the funk of unwashed men. The main living area was tiny and dark, with a wood stove at the center and a chimney going up through the roof. A table and four chairs, all rough and uneven on their legs, sat in a corner. A doorway led into another room, likely the bedroom. From what she'd seen of the outside of the house, it would be small as well. She stood awkwardly and pinched her nose, unsure of what to do.

Jack glared at her as he tossed his hat onto a peg by the door. "Whatcha doin'? We're hungry—get to cookin'!"

She drifted to the table, realizing there was a small pantry against the wall behind it. A quick search revealed some potatoes, onions and salt pork. It seemed Jack intended her to earn her keep. And she knew she had to do as he said—at least until she'd found a way to escape. She unearthed a frying pan and before long had the ingredients sizzling on the stove.

She was grateful for the work she'd done at the saloon, or she wouldn't have known even how to light the fire in the stove, let alone make a meal. Mrs. Patterson had been a great source of knowledge on so many subjects, and she'd soaked up as much as she could while helping her.

The men sat and began a game of cards. Jack pulled out a bottle of whiskey, which was passed around freely as they played. Each exclaimed with sorrow at a loss, or shouted in delight at a victory periodically. Hattie did her best to ignore them. Perhaps if she kept quiet and out of their way, they'd get drunk and forget all about her.

When the food was done, she piled it onto four plates and set three of them on the table with forks. "Supper's ready," she said quietly, wringing her hands. She hated to interrupt them—it went against her plan of not being noticed—but what choice did she have?

The men didn't respond, not even with the food smack in front of them.

Anger rose up in her, sudden as a summer squall. "Suppertime!" she called, this time louder.

The men all looked up at her, and she gasped, her hand covering her mouth. Only now could she clearly see the face of the man who'd ridden with the neckerchief pulled over his face. He smirked at her, laid down his cards and pulled his plate close. "Looks good." He dug the fork into a thick piece of potato.

"Hans!" she exclaimed.

Deputy Hans Bergman grinned at her. "Hello there, Hattie. Nice to see ya again."

Chapter Ten

The clip-clop of horses' hooves on the hard road into town was music to Ed's ears. He'd been gone longer than planned, but he'd finally found homes for each of the children, though some of those were only temporary. He was exhausted, and couldn't wait to reach the cozy apartment above his office, fall into bed and sleep.

He pulled the wagon into the livery and settled the horses. The livery owner was likely already asleep, and he didn't want to disturb the man. Once the horses were taken care of and the wagon stowed away, he ambled down the street and through the rear door of his office. He carried a bowl outside to the water pump to fill with water so he could wash before he retired. His stomach growled with hunger, but he didn't have the energy to fix supper. He'd eat a hearty breakfast the next day.

When he fell into bed, sleep overtook him within moments. The last thought that flitted through his mind was of Hattie. He hoped she'd be glad to see him and couldn't wait to go to her.

His whole body ached the next morning after so many days riding in a wagon and sleeping in barns all over the countryside. He rolled onto his side, ran a hand over his tired eyes and set his feet onto the floor, then stood with a wide yawn and arms stretched high. The sun was out and the day looked bright, with only a hint of cool in the air to announce that fall was on its way.

He dressed quickly and trotted downstairs to open the office. He found it strange that Hans wasn't in yet—the man was an early riser and usually beat him to work. Lee was nowhere to be seen either. He frowned, tugged his hat from the peg by the door and stepped out onto the porch, peering left and right with a squint. The first thing he wanted to do was call at the Roan Horse Saloon—he'd get a chance to see Hattie and order a big breakfast at the same time.

When he saw Lee striding toward him, his face broke into a wide grin. He slapped Lee on the back and rested his hands on his hips. "How's it goin', *amigo*?" he asked.

Lee scratched his chin. "*Oye*, boss. When you get in?"

"Last night. I'm just heading over to the saloon for breakfast." Then Ed noticed Lee wasn't meeting his gaze. "What is it, *compadre*? And where's Hans?"

"I not know where Hans is. But *Señorita* Stout told me that he beat *Señorita* Sweeney. And now *Señorita* Stout…she's missing."

His heart fell into his stomach. "What? What do you mean 'missing'?"

"She came to the office yesterday looking for you. I told her you would be back soon. She told me about Hans and *Señorita* Sweeney, and she left. She seemed upset, but I no think too much of it—you know how women are sometimes. But I was just at the saloon to talk to *Señorita* Sweeney, and *Señora* Yancey said *Se-ñorita* Stout did not come home yesterday."

Ed's head spun with the news. Where could she be? "Did Sally check to see if her things were still in her closet?"

Lee shook his head. "Ohhh, I no think to ask! I came here right away to see if you were back. I thought you would want to know."

Ed strode off toward the saloon, Lee trotting along beside him. "Thanks, Lee. And you have no idea where Hans is?"

"No. He disappear the day you left town. At first I thought it was just one of his…you know." Lee mimed drinking from a bottle. "But he is still not back, no one knows where he is, and what happened with *Señorita* Sweeney…" He trailed off into mumbled Spanish—a prayer, a curse, Ed couldn't tell.

Ed's nostrils flared. He'd just returned to town and already he had two missing persons. Where could Hans be? Had something happened to both he and Hattie? He pushed through the swinging doors and into the saloon. "Sally?"

She smiled from behind the bar, her blonde hair tucked loosely behind her ears. "Sheriff Milton, yer back. How good to see ya—we've missed ya 'round these parts." She set two shot glasses on the bar and poured whiskey into each. "Take a seat, gentlemen."

"We're not here to drink." Ed marched to the bar and rested his hands on the counter. "Where's Hattie? Lee said she didn't come back to the saloon yesterday. Have you seen her?"

Sally shrugged. "Nope."

"Did you check her room?"

Her eyes narrowed. "No, Sheriff, I didn't think of that, simple as I am," she remarked sarcastically.

He crossed his arms. "I meant, did you notice whether her things were still in her room?"

"Let's go and see, I guess." Sally waddled from behind the bar, the ever-present dishtowel over one shoulder. Ed followed her up the stairs and along the narrow hallway. She stopped at a paint-chipped door and raised a hand to knock. A voice called softly for her to come in, and she pushed the door open and poked her head through. After a few words with the occupant, she opened the door wide and motioned for Ed and Lee to follow her inside. "Sheriff, Lee, you know Daisy."

Ed strode directly to the closet and flung the door open. "Are these her gowns?" he asked Daisy, who sat on the edge of her bed, her eyes downcast. Then he got a good look at her and shivered. "What the...? Did Hans do that?" He hurried to her side and squatted in front of her to take a closer look.

"I told Deputy Lee, I'm fine. I just had a little accident." Daisy shifted away from him on the bed.

"Accident? You look like you were in a bar fight!" He stood, clenching his fists at his sides, and glared at Sally. "You let this happen?"

Sally stared at him defiantly. "Don't get on yer high horse with me, Ed Milton—he's yer deputy!" She flounced off in a swirl of skirts and petticoats.

Ed frowned. And Hans was nowhere to be found. "You can tell us the truth, Daisy. We'll protect you, I promise."

"Ye will?" Daisy seemed surprised.

"We will. He'll never do this to you again."

Daisy stared at her stocking feet, gathering her courage. "It was him. It was Hans. And it ain't the first time, neither."

Ed swallowed hard and his fingers twitched. He'd like to get his hands on his deputy, but he had to focus on finding Hattie first and worry about Hans later. The deputy had probably skipped town, afraid of what Ed would do when he found out about Daisy's injuries. He knelt in front of Daisy again. "Do you know where Hattie is? I really need your help—she's missing and I'm worried about her."

She raised red eyes to meet his. "If I knew where she was, I'd tell you. But she never came home yesterday. She was just supposed to be gone for a few minutes— she went to find you, then she'd come back. When she didn't, I just assumed the two of you were together… but when she never showed up for supper or bedtime, I knew somethin' was wrong…" Tears rolled down her cheeks and she sniffled.

"Thank you, Daisy." Ed stood quickly and marched to the door. "Let's go, Lee."

Lee ran after him down the hall. "Where we going, boss?"

"Gather a posse together. We're going looking for Hattie."

Lee paused, then called after him. "But we don't know where she is. Where are we going to look?"

"Just do as I say—I'll meet you back at the office." As he left the saloon, Ed considered the possibilities, but try as he might, he couldn't think of a reason for her sudden disappearance, not with all her belongings still at the saloon. As he crossed the street his stomach growled, but once again he ignored it. Breakfast would have to wait.

* * *

Hattie rolled over on the hard boards with a groan. She rubbed the sleep from her eyes, felt a tug and heard a jangle. Jack had chained her to a support beam in the grimy, damp cabin he'd taken her to. She opened her eyes and stared up at the patchy roof above, grateful at least for fine weather. But still, she was a captive.

Her arm ached where Jack's fingers had bruised her and her back throbbed in the places he'd struck. Tears pricked her eyes as memories flooded back. She'd hoped to win Jack's trust so he might let down his guard and she could escape. After supper, when the men had returned to their drinking and card-playing, she'd tried to sneak out the back door, but Jack had caught sight of her out of the corner of his eye, beaten her repeatedly and chained her to the post. The reality of her situation now clear, she'd cried herself to sleep on the cold wood floor.

Now she took a slow, deep breath, sat up beside the post and crossed her legs beneath her skirts. The men must still be asleep. They'd retired sometime in the night—she'd stirred as she heard them clamber drunkenly into the adjoining room—and now she could hear snoring emanating from within.

Hattie tugged at the chain, pulling her wrist bindings taut, and wriggled her hands, opening and closing her fists and twisting them around, searching for a weak point. The noise of the links rubbing against each other would be enough to waken a sober man, and she grabbed at them to silence them, but their snoring continued. She narrowed her hands and pulled hard against one binding, grimacing, her mouth opened in a silent scream.

One hand came free! The act left ugly red welts on her skin, but she still grinned with delight and began to work on the other wrist. The pain almost made her sob, but she wasn't about to give up. Finally her other hand slipped free—she held it close, rocking back and forth with her eyes squeezed shut until the pain ebbed.

She looked up and her shoulders slumped.

Hans stood in front of her, leaning against the frame of the bedroom door. His shirt was untucked, his hair stuck out in all directions, and he looked her up and down with bloodshot eyes. "Well, well. Aren't you clever? We'll have to make sure to tighten those bindings the next time. That husband of yours is too soft—didn't want to hurt you. But I'm not worried about that."

He walked over, grabbed her wrists and yanked her to her feet. She cried out in pain, and he pushed her against the cold hard wall. "There's no use trying to escape, m'lady. Not a soul around these parts for miles. No one to help you. You'd have a better chance of being eaten by a bear or starving to death than getting back to town. So fix it in your mind to stay put. Got it?"

She nodded, whimpering at the stinging in her wrists.

He grinned and released her, but didn't back away. "So here we are, all alone. Jack won't be awake for hours yet. It's just you and me."

His breath stank, and she couldn't help but notice his blackened teeth beneath his swooping mustache. She smiled at him, put her hands against his chest… then shoved him backward as hard as she could. "You keep your hands off me!" she yelled.

Hans stumbled, then caught himself and laughed.

When he grabbed her again, his fingers were like pincers on her arms and she struggled beneath his grasp. His eyes narrowed and he shook her hard, smacking her head against the wall. Her vision blurred.

The click of a hammer being cocked broke the silence. Then a gravelly voice rasped, "Step away from my wife, Hans."

Hans released her and spun around. She could see Jack over his shoulder, and the shotgun Jack was pointing at Hans' head.

"What do ya think yer doin'?" Jack snarled.

Hans raised his hands in mock surrender and stepped toward the gun. "Just caught her trying to get away. She got out of the chains and was trying to escape again, Jack."

Jack's eyes clouded with uncertainty. His gaze rested on Hattie's face, and she felt the blood drain from it under his glare. "That so? So ya didn't learn yer lesson last night." He lowered the barrel of the gun slowly and straightened his back. "Mind ya don't try it again, girl, or ya'll be regrettin' it. Tie her up." He turned and walked out the front door, slamming it shut behind him.

Hans turned on her, his face red with anger. "He'll get his when the time comes. And so will you." He grabbed her wrist and dragged her back to the pole. When he fastened the chains around her wrists this time, he cinched them so tight her fingers began to go numb. With a smirk, he went out the door as well.

Hattie winced and leaned against the post, tears smarting in her eyes. How could she ever escape?

Would she spend the rest of her life with these men? Would they kill her? The remnant of hope hidden in her heart since her capture evaporated, and she wept.

Chapter Eleven

Ed wiped his face with his handkerchief and sighed deeply as the rest of the posse picked its way up the winding trail between the trees behind him. They'd been searching for Hattie for a week now, and the rest of the men were tiring of it. They were done with the daily hunting trips and just wanted to spend an evening at home with their families. None believed they'd find her.

Except him.

Where was she? She could be holed up anywhere between Coloma and the Canadian border by now. There were miles of woods in every direction, and they hadn't even crossed the river to search the other side. And he hadn't heard a thing about his deputy's whereabouts. At this stage, everyone was certain Hans had played some part in Hattie's disappearance—including Ed.

He made up his mind. They'd investigate the crest of this hill, then head back to town. It would be dark before they got there as it was, and some of the men were already complaining among themselves when they thought he couldn't hear. He knew he couldn't continue asking them to help him search.

But he couldn't give up. If it came down to it, he'd keep searching for Hattie on his own. She had to be somewhere—she couldn't simply vanish into thin air...

A wispy trail of smoke near the summit of the hill signaled the presence of a cabin. His eyes narrowed—he wasn't aware of anyone living in this area. It was possible a settler had moved in. He didn't know the whereabouts of every settler in the area, it was too big a space and too many people were staking claims every season for him to keep track of. But why would anyone settle at the top of a hill, where you couldn't farm or graze?

He signaled the rest of the crew toward the smoke and urged his horse forward to lead the way. Soon they came upon the cabin. A few tins and scraps were scattered around the clearing where it stood, and three horses stood under a lean-to beside the structure, sheltering from the heat. It didn't look like a family home—no garden, no wagon and no animals besides the horses.

The sheriff held up a hand to halt the posse's progress, then climbed down to hide behind the thick trunk of an oak. He peered around the tree, squinting through the falling darkness. There was movement inside the house—from what he could see through the narrow window, there looked to be at least two men inside.

He crept over the dusty ground, knees bent and head low, then stopped still beside the window. With a quick, smooth movement he grabbed the window ledge and peeked over the sill, then quickly he lowered himself back to the ground and scampered back to join the rest of the men.

Lee stepped forward to hand him the reins to his mount. "What you see, boss?" he whispered.

Adrenaline coursed through Ed's veins. "It's them. Hattie's inside on the floor—I think she's chained to something. And I saw Hans, dozing in a chair. There's at least one other man, but I can't be sure how many exactly. There are two rooms and I could only see into one."

Lee's eyes flew wide. "*Dios mio*—Hans did kidnap her!"

"Looks that way." They mounted up and rode back to join the rest of the group. "All right, listen up," Ed hissed to the others. "There's two men, maybe more, and a woman in there. Yes, the woman is Hattie Stout—she's chained up in the middle of the room. There's another room behind it, possibly more men in there. They're definitely armed. And one of the men is Hans Bergman."

There was a general murmur in the group at his revelations.

Ed gave orders for where each man should stand and how they'd enter the cabin, and they all dismounted to tie their horses to the trees. As each man checked and readied his weapons, Ed crept back toward the cabin, leading the way forward. He moved slowly up the stairs and across the porch, shotgun in hand. He tried the front door, and found it wasn't locked. He pushed it open gently as he cocked the hammer on his weapon.

The door creaked as it swung open. Hans jumped to his feet and dove through the bedroom doorway just as Ed's shotgun blasted a hole in the chair he'd been sleeping on.

Hattie screamed, just as the rest of the posse stormed

the cabin. A shot resounded from the second room and the other men all took cover. But Ed crawled across the floor to Hattie, who was weeping with her head against the planks. He put an arm around her and held her.

She glanced up at him, her eyes wide with terror as shots rang out around them. "Ed... I can't get these off," she whimpered, holding up her wrists.

He nodded and tugged at her bonds, but they were fixed too tightly. He pulled again, harder this time, but still no luck. Leaning his head against hers so she could hear him, he said, "I'm sorry, Hattie, but it's going to hurt. I've got to get you out of here—you might be shot if you stay. Can you manage it?"

She nodded and shut her eyes tight as she held out her wrists toward him.

He bit down on his lower lip, took a grip and pulled. He could see the pain written on her face, but she didn't utter a sound. Finally, the chain slipped from one hand, dripping blood as it clanged to the floor beside her. He quickly removed the other one, then took her in his arms and carried her outside as the shooting continued behind them.

He ran back to the horses and set her in Fire's saddle. "Wait here—I'll be back soon. There's a shotgun if you need it." He pointed to the weapon stowed in a scabbard on his saddle.

She grasped his arm as he tried to head back. "Please don't leave me, Ed," she pleaded.

"I promise, I'll come back for you." He reached up to cup her cheek, running his fingertips over her tear-streaked skin.

"All right." She sat straight and lifted her chin, taking Fire's reins in her hands.

He grinned at her strength, then ran back to the cabin.

As he skirted the outside of the structure, he pulled one pistol from its holster. He reached a back window, stood beside it for a moment, then leaned inside and shot. Jack Miller dropped onto a low bed with a cry and Hans spun around to face Ed, shooting through the opening. Ed ducked and the bullet whizzed past his head. He popped up again and took aim, firing at the fleeing Hans, who leaped behind an overturned chest of drawers.

Another man, with a long red beard, sped by the window while Ed pulled his other pistol, joining Hans. Ed fired and fired again, splintering the wood panels in the sturdy chest. But as he reloaded again, the two men burst out from behind it, shooting wildly at the rest of the posse holed up in the living room and barreling out the back door, desperate to get away.

Ed sprinted around the outside of the cabin in time to see the men running hard for the tree line toward the posse's horses. *Hattie!* He ran after them, heart pounding and legs pumping until he reached the tree line. He slowed and crept cautiously into the woods. It wouldn't do to run into an ambush, and he couldn't see far enough ahead of himself to tell where the outlaws now were.

The woods were quiet save for the swish of branches in the evening breeze. His ears fairly burned to hear something, anything, to tell him which way the scoundrels had run. If they'd taken the horses, he'd hear them crashing through the undergrowth.

One by one the other men from the posse joined him. They were breathing hard, their eyes wide as they glanced around them. The unmistakable click of a shotgun's hammer reached their ears through the hush. Ed froze and the others stopped still behind him. He could see the horses up ahead, with Hattie.

The corners of Ed's mouth twitched up into a grin. Hattie was still seated on his mount, his shotgun raised to her shoulder as she peered down the sights. The end of the weapon was trained directly at Hans' chest, and both he and the man with the red beard had their hands into the air.

Ed laughed and ran forward, reholstering his pistols and pulling out handcuffs as he went. "You two are under arrest," he shouted behind the men. He cuffed Hans, then did the same for the other man.

The red-bearded one looked at Hans and grumbled, "I told Jack she'd only make trouble for us. Told him a hundred times. Didn't I?"

"Shut up," Hans grunted.

Ed smiled at Hattie. One glance revealed a steely determination in her eyes he'd never seen before. She still had the gun aimed at Hans, her gaze unwavering. He walked to her side and laid a hand gently on the gun's muzzle. "You did good, Hattie. You can put that away now."

She lowered the weapon and looked at him, her eyes narrowed, then relaxed with a long sigh.

"When did you learn to use a shotgun?" he asked, tipping his hat back.

"Father was member of a dove-shooting club on Long Island. Sometimes he'd take me along—much to Mother's disapproval," she added.

He chuckled. "Well, your father has my thanks. If it weren't for you, they would have gotten away." He watched Lee and the other men saddle the outlaws' horses and strap each prisoner, handcuffed and sullen, onto their backs. They had to tie Jack Miller in securely—he was bleeding from a wheezing chest wound, and couldn't hold himself up.

Neither, as it turned out, could Hattie, now that the crisis was over. When Ed saw her sway in the saddle, he opened his arms and caught her with a grunt. He lowered her to the ground as her eyelids flickered open. "Water," she whispered. Then her eyes fell shut again, two dark crescents against pale cheeks.

He took the canteen from the saddlebag and held it to her lips. She slurped at it, gulping it down. He noted the dark circles beneath her eyes, the scratch on her cheek, the purple bruising on her temple and down her neck. Her dress was torn in several places, with buttons hanging loose, and he could see another bruise near her elbow where the fabric of her sleeve had fallen away. He bit his lower lip and felt the blood rush to his head. What had they done to her? If only he hadn't taken so long to find her, he could have prevented all of this.

Her eyes fell open again and she tried to sit up. He helped her to her feet, then looped an arm beneath her legs and gently lifted her back onto his horse. Her head lolled and she shuddered as he moved behind her and wrapped an arm tightly around her middle. With the reins in his other hand, he clicked his tongue and Fire set off sedately down the hillside. "All right, boys," he called over his shoulder. "'Bout time we headed home."

The posse sent up a ragged cheer. Lee took charge of the prisoners and the rest of the men helped him shepherd their charges back to town. It was a tired but content crew that trotted into Coloma that evening.

By the time they arrived, Hattie was shivering with

shock, whimpering against his chest. "I'll take you to Sally's—she'll look after you," he whispered into her hair.

"No!" she declared forcefully. "No, not Sally's."

"Well…why not?"

Those four words had sapped most of her energy—her reply was mumbled toward the ground. "She said if I stayed there… I'd have to…just don't take me there."

He raised an eyebrow.

But where would he take her? It would have to be his apartment above the sheriff's office. It'd been a temporary home for him when he first accepted the position. He'd always intended to purchase a patch of land outside town where he could build a cabin, raise chickens and a family, God permitting. But he'd never met a woman he'd consider sharing his life with until now. So he'd stayed in the cramped quarters that stank of stale bread and sweat.

But since Sally's wasn't an option, and the hotels in town were no place for a single woman in bad shape—nor did he feel right leaving her alone—his place would have to do for tonight.

He followed slowly behind Lee and the others down the lamplit street. They dismounted, hauled Hans and the red-bearded outlaw into the sheriff's office and locked them in the jail cells. One of the posse had taken the wounded Jack Miller ahead of the others, and the town doctor was working on him on Hans' desk.

Ed walked Fire behind the office to the stables, where Hattie half-climbed, half-fell into his arms. He carried her in through the back door, past the cells and the prisoners and the doc working to save Jack Miller's sorry life, and upstairs to his apartment.

He set her on her feet just as the apartment door burst open and Daisy barreled through, her face white beneath her bruises. "Is it Hattie? Ye found her! I saw you ridin' by the saloon and came as quick as I could. Is she all right?" She rushed to Hattie's side and stroked the hair back from her forehead with gentle fingertips.

Ed nodded. "I think so. Just a bit bruised and cold." He went to a closet against the wall, pulled out two blankets and a towel and laid them on the bed, then watched the two women whisper together, Daisy's arms tight around Hattie. "I'm gonna let the doc know she's up here. I don't know how long he'll be," he added, carefully pulling the door closed behind him.

He leaned against the door and sighed. The sight of her, so pale and bruised, had filled him with rage, and he'd ridden that dark energy home. But now it was over. The Miller Gang was locked up downstairs. Hattie was in his apartment, alive and safe. And after the last few weeks, he was on the verge of collapse. But his work wasn't done.

He rubbed his face with his hands, his eyes squeezed shut, then headed downstairs.

The doctor had finished treating Jack Miller, who was now asleep on a mat on the floor of his cell, wrapped in a dry blanket. Ed combed his fingers through his sweat-soaked hair in relief. "Hey, Doc. I've got Hattie Stout upstairs. Do you think you could check on her before you leave?"

"Sure thing, Sheriff. Glad you finally found the girl. How's she seem?"

"Bruised, a bit disoriented, but all right… I think." His chest tightened. Who knew what had happened to

her in the last week? "Let me know if there's anythin'
I can do to help?"

The doctor smiled. "I'm sure she'd like some hot
food and something to drink."

Ed grinned, glad to be given a task. He watched the
doctor head upstairs, then hurried outside. He'd see if
Sally would give him some food—and while he was
at it, he could pack up Hattie's things and bring them
back to his place. He put his hat back on and stepped
out into the night.

Chapter Twelve

Hattie pulled the blanket up higher over her shoulder and rolled onto her side. She yawned and rubbed her eyes as the bright California sun peeped beneath the drapes.

She sat up, pulled back the curtain and stared down at the stables below. A coyote trotted through the yard, and she heard the stamp of hooves against the hard ground. One of the horses whinnied, and the wild animal stopped in its tracks, glancing around the yard. Then a dog ran barking across the packed dirt, and the coyote bolted down the lane and disappeared from view, the dog in hot pursuit.

She smiled. It was good to be alive, well and snug in the sheriff's bed. She didn't know how many days it had been since he rescued her, but it must have been several. When she'd first arrived, she'd been so tired, thirsty, hungry and sore she'd slept for the better part of three days before finally feeling somewhat better.

She stretched her arms over her head with another yawn, then swung her feet to the ground and stood with a satisfied sigh. A glance in the looking glass he'd kindly set up for her revealed that most of her bruising was gone now. She frowned as a thought occurred to her—where was he sleeping? She hadn't thought to ask him that.

Daisy snored at her feet, on her back with one arm flung above her head. Her sleeping mat was pushed up close to Hattie's bed. But it already felt like home to her after only a few weeks. Daisy had come to help take care of her that first night, and never left except to go back to the Roan Horse and pack her own things. Now everything the two women owned was piled high in a corner of Ed's small apartment. Ed had done nothing more than arch an eyebrow when he saw it.

She tiptoed around Daisy and poured herself a glass of water from the jug. As she gulped the cool liquid, she couldn't help thinking about what might come next. She fingered the necklace her father gave her, which Ed had recovered from the Miller Gang's cabin. Ed had been so kind to let them use his apartment and eat his food, but they couldn't stay there forever. They'd have to come up with a plan to face the future soon.

At least she didn't have to worry about Jack Miller. From what she understood, he and his fellow outlaws were wanted in several northern California counties and had been sent to Sacramento to stand trial. The man with the red beard had turned out to be Peter Miller, Jack's brother. The cells downstairs stood empty once again and life in Coloma had returned to normal. And most importantly, her petition for annulment had been granted the morning after Jack's capture. She was free of the blackguard forever.

She set the glass back on the table beside the water

jug and dressed slowly, enjoying the summer heat as she sat before the looking glass to fix her hair.

It would be fall soon, her favorite season—at least it had been back in New York. The black trunks of the trees would stand stark and grim in the frosty air as leaves turned red, yellow and orange, then dropped to the ground to coat it like a warm blanket. She'd tug up her coat collar and layer herself with scarves and hats, stockings and boots, or sit before a warm fire, roasting chestnuts and sipping hot coffee or chocolate. She couldn't imagine what fall in California might be like.

She considered how much she missed home—her family, her friends. Why hadn't she heard from any of them? She hadn't received a single letter since she arrived, though she'd sent several. She knew her parents were likely very busy trying to rebuild their name and reputation, not to mention the family fortune. But she'd love to hear from them, just the same.

A quiet knock on the door made her heart skip. She finished buttoning the bodice of her dress, then went to the door and opened it. Ed was standing there, hat in hand and blue eyes sparkling. "Good mornin', Hattie," he said with a grin.

"Good morning, Ed. How are you on this fine day?" In the weeks since she'd been there, she'd come to anticipate the sheriff's daily visits. He always brought her something—a bunch of wildflowers, a book he'd borrowed, a treat from the bakery. Then they'd sit together on the porch swing out front and talk about his day, or hers, their hopes and dreams.

"Just dandy, thank you. And you? Are you feelin' better?"

She laughed. "You ask me that every day. And every

day I tell you yes, I'm feeling much better. Thank you kindly."

He brought his right hand from behind his back and thrust a bunch of colorful flowers toward her with a smile. "Oh, they're beautiful, Ed. Thank you." She took them and smelled their sweet aroma. It wouldn't be long before they'd be gone for the year and she wouldn't see another until spring. She took a glass, filled it with water, set the flowers in it and put them on a table against the far wall, away from the beds.

Ed rested his hand on his hip and leaned against the door jamb. "Would you like to take a walk? I've got a little time before I have to get to work."

She nodded and reached for her bonnet on a peg by the door. As she closed the door behind her, she chuckled at the loud snore that reverberated across the room.

"Daisy's still sleeping?" he asked, as they descended the narrow staircase together.

"Yes, she is. I swear, she could sleep through peak hour at Grand Central Depot." She laughed and took the sheriff's offered arm to walk outside.

The town had woken already, and miners trudged through the streets on their way to the mines. Farmers trundled by in wagons, loaded with bags of seed or other supplies. Children with lunch pails swinging from eager hands hurried toward the schoolhouse on a rise opposite the church, the sun glinting off its newly whitewashed walls.

They wandered in that direction and soon found themselves passing the schoolhouse. Children skipped with ropes, drew in the dirt or chased each other around the building while they waited for the schoolmistress to open the doors and order them inside. Hattie laughed at their antics and the smile didn't leave her face as she soaked up the sunshine. She glanced at Ed, who watched her with interest, his eyes wide and full of passion.

He stopped and took both her hands in his. "Hattie…"

"I don't know if I've thanked you enough for letting Daisy and me stay in your apartment," she interrupted.

He swallowed hard. "Yes, you have. You've thanked me plenty—"

"It's just that I don't know what we would have done if it weren't for you. You've rescued me, given us a place to stay, fed us, taken care of us. And I know it's probably time for us to move on—you've certainly done more than anyone could expect…"

He cut her off, his eyebrows drawn low. "Move on?"

"Well, we can't stay in your apartment forever. I mean, where are you even sleeping?"

"Downstairs, at my desk."

"You see? We've completely displaced you. You should be upstairs in your own bed, in your snug apartment. I feel terrible about it."

He spun away from her, his hands in the air. "But what will you do? Where will you go?" His voice trembled with emotion.

She frowned. "Well, I'm not sure just yet. I had been trying to save to return to New York, but then Sally… you know." Her voice trailed off.

"Yes, I do."

She'd told him all about Sally's ultimatum when he suggested she move back into the Roan Horse a few days after her rescue.

Her head hung low. "Daisy warned me she would

do just what she did, but I didn't believe her. I thought Sally was my friend as well. But she wasn't—she just cares about herself. Hans hurt Daisy, and Sally didn't do anything about it. As long as Hans paid, she didn't care what he did to Daisy…" Her voice broke and tears trailed down her cheeks.

He reached up and brushed them away. "I'm so sorry, Hattie. I should never have suggested you stay there. I thought you'd be fine as a kitchen hand or maid. I don't know why I…well, I just should've found you someplace else. I'm sorry." He wound his arms around her back and pulled her against him.

She sobbed into his shirt, wetting it with her tears. Her hands bunched as fists beneath her chin and she shivered under his touch. The warmth of his chest calmed her soul.

When she'd cried all she could and her body stopped trembling, he tilted up her chin to look at him. His eyes were full of love. She marveled at the lines that ran down his tanned cheeks, ending in soft dimples above his full beard, the ocean of blue in the depths of his eyes and the soft curl that fell dark over his forehead. She exhaled slowly, her gaze never leaving his. They were joined together, soul to soul, by a look that shut out the world.

"There's something I promised to tell you before Jack took me. Do you remember that?"

He nodded.

"I found a way to end my marriage to Jack, as though it never happened. It's all final—remember when Tom Small came by the day after you brought me back? He finished all the paperwork that day. I'm not married to Jack anymore."

His eyes widened and he lifted a hand to rub his beard. "Hattie...then I can say what I've wanted to say for months. I don't want you to leave." His voice was low and soft. "I want you to stay. Forever."

She tilted her head, her eyes narrowed. "Forever? Are you sure, Ed? Forever certainly is a long time." She was teasing, but her heart jitterbugged and she broke out in a cold sweat.

"I sure hope it's a long time, because I never want to be without you. I want to marry you. Will you have me?" His fingers grazed her cheek and traced the outline of her jaw, making her skin tingle.

Before she could help herself she stood on tiptoe to press her lips to his. The softness of his touch, the warmth of his breath, made her pulse race. She pulled away and her gaze flickered over his weathered face.

"Is that a yes?" he whispered.

She smiled and looped a hand around his neck. "Yes! It's a yes!" Then she kissed him again. The world stood still. And this time she didn't pull away.

Chapter Thirteen

Daisy and Hattie walked side by side, arm in arm, down the street. Hattie stared at the night sky overhead, stars sparkling like jewels in an ocean of black. The moon, almost full, hung low and round near the horizon, with the town basking in its unearthly glow.

Tomorrow was her wedding day.

Each time she thought about it, her heart skipped a beat. She was excited, nervous with anticipation and full of joy. Ever since he'd proposed, Ed had been so attentive. He'd purchased a plot of land outside the town limits and spent every spare moment he had erecting a two-room cabin for them to call home. He promised her he'd extend it over time until he'd built her dream home, but she assured him she didn't need anything more. As long as they had each other.

"Are ye ready for tomorrow?" asked Daisy wistfully.

"Mmmm…" Hattie couldn't put the swirl of thoughts in her mind into words.

"Are you sure Ed don't mind me stayin' above the

sheriff's office 'til I find my feet?" asked Daisy, biting her lower lip to still its trembling.

Hattie faced her with a smile and cupped her cheek in a gloved hand. "Yes, of course I'm sure. He won't need it any longer. And anyway, where else would you go?"

Daisy pursed her lips. "Well, long as you're sure."

"I am. And I'll be visiting you all the time. We won't be far away, just a few minutes out of town. And Ed is teaching me how to ride and to hitch up his horse to his wagon so I can come into town whenever I like." She patted Daisy's hand and they continued up the street.

The steady beat of hooves interrupted the still night and Hattie squinted through the darkness. The town was sleeping, apart from the drunken revelers around the saloons at the other end of town. She soon realized it was Ed riding toward them when she saw the long white stripe on Fire's snout. "Ed!" she called, stepping out from the shadows and into the moonlit street.

He waved. Another horse, a white one, trotted behind him, and he pulled her along with a lead. He halted in front of the women and swung down from Fire's back. He patted the white horse affectionately on the neck, then leaned in to kiss Hattie.

Her cheeks burned and she glanced at Daisy, who chuckled softly, her eyes gleaming.

"Hattie, Daisy—how nice to see you lovely ladies. Hattie, I have a gift for you. What do you think—isn't she a beauty?"

Hattie's eyes widened. "She's for me?" She stepped forward and laid a hand on the horse's shoulder. The animal shivered beneath her touch and she stroked the mare's back. "She's lovely. Perfect."

"I figured you'd want to visit town sometimes when I'll have Fire with me, so decided I'd get you a horse of your own. Thought you could call her Ice, since she's white as snow." He grinned and tipped back his hat.

Hattie laughed. "Fire and Ice. Sounds just about right."

"Well, I'd better get her put away in the stable. We can take her out to the new house tomorrow—I've built a stable and yard there already, so they'll have a snug little place to live, just like us." He tipped his hat and climbed back onto Fire. "Oh, I almost forgot. I stopped by the post office earlier today and there was a stack of letters for you."

Hattie's breath caught in her throat. "Really? Oh, I wonder if they're from Mother and Father. I've been waiting to hear from them for so long."

"The postmaster said it looked like they got lost or held up somewhere along the way, since they all arrived at once." He reached into his saddlebag and pulled out the letters, tied together with a piece of string.

Hattie took them and held them up to her face, straining to read in the dull light. Yes, the first one was from Father. She flicked through the pile, there were others in there from her sister Della and Mother as well. "Thank you, Ed." Her voice was heavy her throat tightened.

"I hope it's good news. I'll leave you ladies to it and see you in the morning at church."

Hattie waved goodbye through a veil of tears. She held the letters to her chest as he rode away, with Ice following obediently behind him.

When she got back, she sat on the bed and opened the first letter while Daisy lit a fire and set the kettle to boil on the stove top. She scanned the contents of the first letter, her heart pounding. Father wrote to let her know his name had been cleared and the swindler who stole their fortune would be brought to justice. The next letter was from Mother, asking how she was settling in and why they hadn't heard from her yet. She said that they'd moved into a modest house and were setting up a new life together with her brothers Tommy and Danny.

She skimmed through several more letters. Her mother exclaimed over the correspondence she'd sent them and all the events she'd relayed to them about Jack Miller and the saloon. Both parents begged her to return to New York as quickly as possible. One letter even contained the money she'd need for a train ticket home, and each was more concerned and frantic than the last. Finally, there was one from Della letting her know she was pregnant and intended to visit New York the following year.

When she'd read them all, her eyes were tired and swollen from crying, her voice hoarse and her throat raw. Daisy had joined her on the bed to listen while Hattie read them out loud, sipping the steaming coffee Daisy had brewed.

Once she was done Hattie sat staring at the opposite wall. "All this time, I could have gone home. I could have been in New York with my family, only the letters were lost between here and there." Her voice broke and she covered her face with her hands.

Daisy patted her leg silently.

Hattie spun to face her, eyes wide and heart pounding. "I could go home now! I don't have to stay here—

I could take the stagecoach tomorrow." She stood and paced the breadth of the small room.

"Aye…but what about Ed? You're supposed to marry him tomorrow." Daisy wrapped both hands around her coffee mug.

Hattie blanched. She couldn't leave Ed. He'd be devastated. And how would she feel leaving him behind and returning to New York? Part of her screamed that she should leave before anything else bad happened, but her heart ached. She loved him. She knew then that if she left and went home, she'd feel empty inside. Life without Ed wouldn't be the way it was before. She couldn't live without him, didn't want to live without him. She couldn't go home.

She sighed and lowered herself slowly back onto the bed beside Daisy, who rested an arm around her shoulders. "I can't leave Ed."

"But will you be happy here?" asked Daisy, laying her coffee cup on the bedside table.

Hattie pulled a handkerchief from her skirt pocket and blew her streaming nose with it. "I don't know. Ever since I arrived, terrible things have happened to me. So I suppose that's made me dislike the place more than I really should. After Ed proposed, I resigned myself to living here, but given the chance… I'd rather go home. Just not without Ed. Oh dear, what should I do?"

"You should talk to him about it."

Hattie leaped to her feet. "Yes, of course. I should talk to Ed." She hurried out the door.

Daisy's voice followed her down the staircase. "Where are ye going? I didn't mean right now!" But Hattie didn't stop until she was out the front door and realized she didn't know where he was. She couldn't very well search for him in the dark on her own.

A sound in the office behind her caught her ear. She crept back inside and there he was, sleeping soundly on a mat on the floor beneath his desk, just as he had for weeks now.

She tiptoed over to him, but couldn't bear to wake him. They'd talk tomorrow. Gazing down on him, she resisted the urge to comb her fingers through his thick hair. He looked so peaceful, so vulnerable lying there. She couldn't leave him. No, she'd marry this man, even if it meant staying in a dirty little mining town the rest of her days.

As she rose to leave, his voice stopped her. "Hattie? Everythin' all right? What's wrong?" He sat up and rubbed his eyes, then stood and rested both hands on her arms, gazing into her eyes with concern.

"I didn't mean to wake you. I'm sorry." She shook her head and cradled his cheek in her palm.

He drew her close and kissed her forehead. "Never mind that. You've been crying. Tell me, what is it?"

She sighed and closed her eyes for a moment. "It's the letters from back home. Mother and Father have recovered a good deal of their fortune, and they want me to come home. They sent money for the train…"

He took a quick breath and pulled away, pressing his hands to his head. "Home?"

"Yes, New York."

He paced to the wall and back again. "And…?"

"And…" She lifted her chin in determination. "And I'm marrying you tomorrow. So I suppose it doesn't matter."

He took her face between his hands and gently

kissed each cheek. "Oh my darlin' Hattie. If you want to go back to your folks, I'm not gonna be the man that stands in your way."

She shook her head slowly, encased between his palms. "I want to marry you. It's just that…"

"What? What is it, my sweet?"

"It's this town! It's so harsh and ugly and mean, and ever since I got here I've endured hardship and cruelty. I don't know what to do. I want to go home, but I want to marry you. I'm confused…" She burst into tears and buried her face in his shirt.

He stroked her hair with one hand, pulling her closer with the other. "Dear sweet Hattie. You should do what you want to. But before you make your decision, can I show you somethin'?"

She pulled away to meet his gaze, a frown drawing her eyebrows low. "Yes, I suppose."

He smiled tiredly and strode to the door. As he put his hat on, he held the door open for her. "After you, my darlin'."

She waited on a hard bench by the door while Ed fetched the wagon. Fire and Ice trotted from the lane with necks arched and hooves springing high. Ed helped her silently into the wagon and they rode beneath the stars for a mile or so. Finally, Ed pulled the wagon off the main road and onto a newly cleared wagon track. They bumped and jostled down it, over a trickling stream, up another hill. Suddenly they emerged into a clearing with a dark cabin close by and a small stable in the distance.

Hattie's eyes widened and she felt her heart lift. "Is this our cabin?" she whispered.

He laughed. "Yes, it is. What do you think?"

She glanced around, taking in the cool swishing of the trees, the cry of a hoot owl overhead, the quiet beauty of the place. She couldn't speak—her throat felt tight and her palms were bathed in sweat.

Ed fetched a lantern from the wagon bed and lit it, then offered Hattie his arm. "Care to take a look inside?"

She nodded, letting her hand nestle in the crook of his arm. He led her into the cabin and set the lantern on a rough-hewn wooden table where it lit up the entire room. The cabin was rustic but warm and inviting. This room was the living area and kitchen, and a door led into another room, their bedroom.

She imagined the two of them living there—sitting in the rockers perched before the fireplace, rocking back and forth together. She thought about the meals they'd share around that table, perhaps with a family of their own. Her heart swelled within her. Nothing in New York could compare to this.

She threw her arms around his neck and showered him with kisses. "Ed, it's perfect. I love it. I can't believe how much work you've put into the place."

He wrapped his arms around her waist and kissed her, his lips exploring hers passionately. When he spoke, his voice was hoarse with passion. "It's for you—all for you. I know we can be happy here, if you'll give us a chance."

She let her eyes wander around the cabin and smiled. "Yes, we will be happy here."

The bells from the church steeple rang out over Coloma. When the sound faded, Hattie ran her hands over her hair, smoothing it back against her head as nerves made her stomach flip. She stood with Daisy outside the chapel, listening to the piano inside playing the tune she would glide down the aisle to.

"Time to go, macushla." Daisy patted her shoulder, her eyes filling with happy tears.

Hattie swallowed hard and nodded. "Yes." She lifted her skirts with one hand, the other clutching a bunch of wildflowers Ed had scavenged from the fields around town. He'd vowed she'd have a bouquet to carry on her wedding day. She glanced down at it through tears— he was always so good to her.

When she reached the stairs to the chapel, a fluttering of wings caught her eye. At least a dozen small white butterflies floated above the lilac bushes that hedged the church entrance. She exclaimed in delight and dropped her skirts to lift her hand beneath one. Its tiny feet alit on her open palm, and it stepped daintily across before fluttering back into the air above her.

"Beautiful, ain't they?" declared Daisy, her voice thick with emotion.

"So beautiful." Hattie closed her eyes for a moment, thanking God for His provision, then walked gracefully up the stairs and through the doors.

When she saw Ed waiting for her at the end of the aisle, the crowd of townsfolk lining the pews faded away. Once again, it was only them—Ed and she, held together by a gaze that was filled with electricity, hope and love.

She reached him and gave him her hand. He held it between his, and together they turned to face the reverend. As they said their vows, she imagined their future as man and wife. Days spent in Coloma, evenings by the fire in their cozy cabin, maybe a trip to New

York around Christmas so he could meet her family. A whole lifetime with nothing but each other and the children they might one day be blessed with.

She couldn't wait for it to begin.

When her new husband kissed her, peace filled her soul and her legs quivered beneath her. No matter what the future brought, she knew that it would be better with him by her side. She looped her arms around his neck to deepen the kiss that signified their union together, forever, as one.

* * * * *

Keep reading for an excerpt from Pearl *by Vivi Holt.*

Chapter One

Southeastern Arizona Territory, March 1888

Harold Carmichael stooped over the cradle, using his worn fingertips to push rock and sand around beneath the cool water's surface. His eye caught a flash of gold, and he pinched it out with his finger and thumb, grinned and stuck it in a small sack attached to his belt. He dashed the remaining sludge back into the river, took a step forward and scooped up another panful of silt and water.

The rock he sat on seemed to grow colder and harder by the minute and a sharp protrusion stabbed into his right buttock. He stood and straightened, rocking the handle and watching the water slide back and forth in the cradle and sending shafts of rainbow light flashing against the brown of his stained shirt.

Noise from the Mammoth Mine, a cracking and thudding, resounded in the distance. He frowned and tilted his hat back with one hand. Dang mining companies—always swooping in whenever there was a sniff of gold, taking the claim and everything in it away from the small-time prospectors. Didn't seem right somehow.

The cry of a muleteer and the faint crack of a whip sailed through the still air, echoing over the river. A twenty-mule team hauled the gold to the mill, then hurried back for more every weekday. He'd seen them do it, his eyes had gone wide with surprise. He'd been there before the mule teams, before the hordes of men descended on the place. Didn't that count for anything? How could a man compete with a setup like the one they had over at Mammoth now?

He rocked the cradle back and forth once more, watching gold flecks fall through to the bottom of the contraption. All that was left for him and the other men standing in knee-deep water or seated beside him along the riverbank were these tiny specks of metal. Not enough for a man to live on, never mind support a family—though the days of raising littl'uns were far behind him now. Still, he'd always held out hope that one day he'd find the largest nugget in the history of the San Pedro River.

"Hey, Harry—you 'bout done for the day?" Murdoch's gravelly voice broke through the chatter of water running over the smooth rounds stones fifty yards downstream.

Harold glanced up at the streaks of gold and pink that painted the horizon beyond the dusty rise, nodded and grunted in assent.

"Thought we might try out that moonshine you been workin' on…" Murdoch continued, his voice turning to a whine that made Harry's eyes roll back in his head. Murdoch was always going on about moonshine. He'd drink up his own by noon and spend the rest of the day feeling around for someone else to satiate his thirst.

"Fine, but you're bringing the food." He glanced at Murdoch beneath lowered brows and grunted at the man's toothless grin. At least someone was happy. He'd barely found a lick of gold today, and it seemed each day was worse than the one before. He should give it up—that's what his wife had told him the day she walked out three years earlier. But he just couldn't.

He knew he'd likely die there alone, in his worn clothes and sun-baked skin on the shores of the San Pedro. It was time to go, to move on. Maybe he should try Los Angeles. Or the gold fields near Sacramento, though word was they'd dried up decades ago. But maybe…

Murdoch made a strangled sound, and Harold looked up from his cradle. "What is it?"

Murdoch didn't hear him. He left his cradle leaning to one side and leaped up the bank, still making that strange sound.

Harold's eyes followed Murdoch's stare as he slowly stood. He raised a hand to shield his gaze from the setting sun's glare burning the tops of the bushes on the riverbank. It was hard to see anything with the sun like that in your face—he saw only the fire of orange and yellow with flashes of white.

What was that?

There was a creature—gold, red, orange, he couldn't say. It was moving fast, then stopped. He squinted against the light and frowned.

Murdoch was moving now, shouting something like, "It's a ghost, with a wee rider!"

That couldn't be right. It clearly wasn't a ghost—

Harold could see it with his own two eyes. And if it were a ghost, would it look different? He wasn't sure—he'd never witnessed a ghost before—but he assumed it would be misty-like or making some kind of eerie sound. This one didn't—it rushed through the brush and undergrowth with the rustle any creature would make.

But it wasn't any creature he'd ever seen, nor wanted to. It was strange-looking, with wild eyes, a long neck, legs that stretched higher than a man was tall and a horribly distorted body. And what was that on the creature's back? It looked like a man, a rider with a whip in his hand and a blood-chilling grin.

Harold scurried up the bank to the canvas satchel where he'd stowed his things and retrieved his shotgun, leaning against a gray tree branch beside the bag. He took aim at the creature, which had dropped its nose to the ground and appeared to be sniffing, or grazing. His gaze fixed, he bent at the knees and crept forward, anxious to get a closer look. It was ragged and wild-looking, and his heart pounded out a steady rhythm as he looked it over.

Closer now, he could see the rider more clearly. The creature shifted, making the rider's head loll precariously to one side, its empty eye sockets seeming to glare directly at him!

Harold shouted in dismay and squeezed the trigger, the gun's recoil against his shoulder making him take a step backwards. The creature took off at a run, its rider bouncing wildly on its back and dropping something in its haste. Another shot rang out, this time from Murdoch's weapon. He cried in dismay when he missed as well. The two men ran after the disappearing creature, guns pointing skyward.

Harold stopped as he drew close to the thing the creature left behind and approached it carefully, his eyes wide. Murdoch followed two steps behind. "What is it?" he asked, gasping.

Harold tugged his hat off and held it against his chest, his eyes squeezed shut. He shook his head from side to side, as if that would make the sight go away.

"What?" asked Murdoch, peering around him. Then he covered his mouth and reeled backward with a retching cough.

Harold opened his eyes slowly and squatted beside what was clearly a human head. Empty eye sockets made dark shadows in the skull, and a shock of reddish hair and remnants of a beard still covered patches of the chin and cheeks. He put his hat back on and backed away. What kind of creature could it have been but a ghost—a red ghost? What else would carry a skeleton rider on its back, dropping half-rotted skulls as it went?

April 1888

Pearl Stout gulped the mouthful of water that remained in the tin cup. She peered out across the arid landscape, wrinkling her nose at the dust that had already caused her to sneeze a dozen times in the past hour. She handed the cup back to Stan, the boy who rode up front beside Sam Smothers the stagecoach driver. She'd learned his name because of every time Sam shouted at him, which was often: "Staaaaaan!" She giggled at the thought of Sam's wide-open mouth, his missing front teeth and his wobbling belly protruding over the belt pulled too tight beneath it.

Then the truth of her journey hit her again, as it had

so many times since she'd set out weeks ago from New York City. She was on her way to be married to a man she'd never met, who lived on the frontier in a place called Tucson. What kind of a name was that? Sam said through a mouthful of bread when they'd stopped for lunch that they were close, but that was two hours ago.

Still, it wouldn't be long until she saw the town that would become her home and the man who'd be her husband.

She took a long, slow breath and frowned. How could her parents do this to her? They'd never given her a choice—if they had, of course she'd have told them she wanted to stay in New York. It was where she was raised, where her family and friends lived. It was home. But they'd ignored all her pleas to let her stay. Her mother hadn't even had the nerve to face her—she'd hidden in her room and made her older sister Della take her meals upstairs to her so she wouldn't have to admit to sending her children away.

Her father Septimus Stout was a hard, determined man, and he'd glared over his newspaper at her when she questioned his decision. When she began to beg to stay, he'd harrumphed, told her it was too late for that, folded his paper under his arm and stalked from the room. She'd cried herself to sleep that night.

When she woke the next morning, she made a decision. She might not get to decide the course of her life, but she could determine how she behaved. And she'd be tarred and feathered before she'd let her parents see her cry again. She hated them in that moment, and when she boarded the westbound train she didn't even bid them farewell. She'd squared her shoulders, picked up her carpetbag and reticule, and marched into the carriage without so much as a glance back.

"Time to go, folks!" called Sam, hiking his pants up with both hands and patting his generous stomach with a smile.

Pearl stood slowly and smoothed her skirts with her gloved hands. Beneath her boots, a picnic rug lay wrinkled over the hard red ground, dusty footprints tracked across its surface. She sighed with frustration. It seemed they would all be covered in dust before the day was through. The coach, the luggage, her clothing, everything had a fine layer of brown that settled whenever the wind fell or movement ceased.

Her heart lurched and her gut roiled. She didn't know the man she'd spend the rest of her life with, but she felt a burning anger deep inside just at the idea of him. Who was he to demand she marry him? Wasn't it her choice who she invited into her life? Wasn't she a grown woman? Well, if you counted a seventeen-year-old as a grown woman, which it seemed her parents did. They presumed her old enough to marry a stranger, which she figured meant she was old enough to make her own choices.

But if she didn't marry him, what then? She had barely enough money left to buy a meal. Her father had been generous enough to give her an allowance for the journey, but nothing more. Maybe he worried his daughters might try to back out of the arrangement if given too much. Or maybe he really didn't have the money any longer.

As she made her way to the stagecoach, her eyes widened at the thought—could it really be true? Her father, the successful businessman, investor and land developer, had lost it all? He said so, but she'd closed herself off to anything he said as soon as he told her and her older sisters they were to be mail-order brides. Her mother had confirmed his words, then left in a bustle of skirts and a rush of tears to let them process it all alone.

Septimus Stout and his brother and business partner Ulysses had lost their businesses to a swindler, who'd also sullied their names in the process. They'd soon lose the house, the servants, everything. It was difficult for her to imagine her parents and brothers reduced to a life of poverty. And where would they go? Where would they live?

She shook her head and stepped up into the coach, settling carefully on the leather seat. Until that moment, she'd only considered her own plight. Now she began to imagine what the others might be going through. Her sisters Della and Hattie had been shipped off before her to meet their husbands in various parts of the West. And she remembered hearing her parents whisper something about her cousins Effie, Minnie and Lula sharing the same fate. But what about the rest? What would become of her brothers?

Her stomach lurched, and she linked her fingers together to rest her hands on it.

The rest of the group crowded into the coach with her. She pressed herself against the window frame as a large woman in long pants and a man's shirt and hat squeezed in beside her. She offered the woman a tight smile. "Not long to go now," she chirped, then winced. The woman made her nervous.

The woman glowered at her through wide-set brown eyes. "Hmph!"

Pearl tried again. "I think I caught your name earlier—was it Bella?"

The woman crossed muscular arms over her generous bosom. "Belle."

"Belle…that's a lovely name."

Belle raised one eyebrow. "And you are?"

Pearl swallowed hard. "I'm Pearl."

"Nice to meetcha." She nodded, the short tight curls on her head unmoving.

"You too."

"You stoppin' in Tucson?" asked Belle, her face softening. She pronounced it *TOO-sahn*, leaving the "c" silent. Was that how it was said?

"I am. And you?"

"Yep. This here's my brother Pip. We're from Richmond, Virginia. How 'bout you?"

Pearl pursed her lips. She hated to tell her story. So far, she'd only told it to the driver before they left, and he'd looked at her with pity in his milky eyes, whistling through the gap where his missing teeth should've been. In that moment she realized just how far she'd come down in the world. "Well, I'm from New York City."

The wagon set off at a slow trundling pace, making the passengers shift. Pearl clutched the windowsill tight to keep from flying into Belle's generous lap.

"That so?" Belle unfolded her arms, her eyes lit up like sparks from a campfire. "I always wanted to go there." She turned to her brother and jammed an elbow into his ribcage. "Ain't you?"

He frowned and rubbed his side. "Huh?"

"Ain't you always wanted to go to New York? This here's Pearl, and she's from New York City!"

"How 'bout that." Pip looked far less impressed. He

pulled his hat down over his eyes and rested his head against the wall of the coach as if to go to sleep.

Pearl's brow furrowed. "Well, maybe one day you'll get there. I don't know if I'll ever go back."

Belle tipped her head to one side, her eyes narrowed. "Whyever not? I'd go there in a flash if I thought I could make it."

"Well, why don't you?" asked Pearl. "You could take the train—that's what I did."

Belle's eyes clouded over. "I don't got no more money. Pip and I gotta get jobs in Tucson, else we'll be beggin' for scraps 'fore long. We worked and saved back home just to get the chance to go West, and Tucson was as far west as we had coin for. We'll work a while, maybe as laborers, see if we like it. Then we might head out to Los Angeles."

Pearl's eyes widened as she sighed. "You're so brave, just deciding to go here or there and making it happen. I can't even imagine." She looked at Belle more closely, noting the woman's smooth brown skin and full lips beneath the layers of grime on her hands and face. It was more than just bravery that made the woman and her brother want to leave Virginia—however rough Tucson might be, it had to be better for Negroes than the stories Pearl had heard coming out of the South.

"Well, you are too! You're on your way to some kind of new adventure in Tucson, ain'tcha?"

Pearl's stomach churned and she ran a hand over her hair. "No, not exactly. I'm…well, my parents decided I should marry a man in Tucson, and I'm going there now to do it. It wasn't my choice. I'm nowhere near as adventurous as you."

Belle didn't reply for a moment, just arched an eyebrow and settled back in her seat to stare out the window. "Think you'll go through with it?" she finally asked.

"Go through with what?"

"Marryin' the man!" she exclaimed, as if indignant at the very idea of doing something she hadn't set her mind to.

"Well, of course. I mean, I hadn't thought about it. Father said I should… I suppose I must."

"Good grief, girl, if you don't wanna do it, ain't no one can make you. You're free, same as Pip and I here are. We weren't always, but we are now and don't we know it!" Belle slapped her thigh as she spoke, her eyes flashing. "You always been free, though it don't seem to me like you understand it. You always do what you're told?"

Pearl grimaced and nodded.

Belle laughed, a hearty chuckle that filled the coach. "Well, now's good a time as any to find your own way, make your own choices. You could be buffaloed into marryin' a man you don't want and raisin' his children. Or you could decide to have an adventure."

"What…kind of adventure?" Pearl asked, her eyebrows pulled low.

Belle leaned closer and whispered, "Any kind you like."

There was a shout from the driver and the stagecoach swayed dangerously to the right, then the left. It stopped suddenly and flung Pearl at the feet of the man opposite her, her face almost in his lap. He'd been snoozing as they rode and his eyes flew open in alarm, focusing on her upturned face. She gasped and struggled to her feet. "So sorry, Mr. Gunderson."

He nodded and straightened his vest. "Never mind, Miss Stout. Never mind."

Before he could say more, there was another cry from outside. Pearl and Mr. Gunderson looked out the window—and her breath caught in her throat. She opened her mouth to scream but no sound came out. Some *thing* was there—it looked almost like a horse, but bigger and deformed. Dust swirled around it as it galloped by the coach. And a headless rider clung to its misshapen back!

The coach horses reared up on their hind legs, whinnying across the desert landscape. Belle screamed as Pearl was hurled back into her seat, her head thudding hard against the frame of the coach. She clutched her head even as the wagon toppled onto its side and she and Belle crashed onto Pip with cries of terror. Mr. Gunderson managed to get on his feet and help pull Pip free.

Between gasps, Pip's voice sounded strangled. "What de debbil was that? Mr. Gunderson, Miss Stout, what you see?"

The noise of the horses trying to regain their footing, clawing and neighing in fright, turned Pearl's stomach. "I don't know," she said with a glance at Mr. Gunderson's pale face. "Some strange beast."

Mr. Gunderson swallowed hard. "With a rider on its back."

Pip's looked from him to Pearl and back again. "What kinda rider?" he demanded.

Pearl shivered. "A headless one."

Historical Note & Author's Remarks

There's something remarkable about a woman who would willingly travel into unknown territory to marry a man she's never met. But in the United States, during the nineteenth century, there weren't many ways for pioneers to find wives, and with the lack of eligible men after the civil war, women in the east often found themselves without beaus—so the mail-order bride industry boomed.

I often wonder about the women who were sent west against their wishes. *Hattie* is the story of a woman, little more than a girl, sent west to marry a man whose only communication with her family was via telegram or letter. A miner, we know he won't be a suitable mate for her but then we find out things are worse than Hattie could possibly have imagined. He's an outlaw, and not only that, he robs the stage coach she's riding in, on her way to meet him.

Sounds improbable, right?

Well, it's not. This story, as with many I write, was inspired by a true tale. Elizabeth Berry was only twenty-two years old when she traveled west to meet bachelor miner Louis Dreibelbis. A school mistress, Elizabeth was to marry Louis, who described himself as a lonely miner in his newspaper ad.

Elizabeth traveled west to avoid becoming a spinster. Apparently twenty-two was approaching old age in the Old West marriage market. Elizabeth packed up her things after a short correspondence with Louis and went to California to marry him. On the way there, her stagecoach was robbed. One of the three robbers allowed her to keep her luggage, which had her wedding dress and all her other belongings for her new life in it. She noticed the man had a ragged scar on one hand.

Later that day, she arrived at her destination. She and Louis went to the justice of the peace to get married. It wasn't until after they exchanged vows, and were pronounced man and wife, that Elizabeth thought she recognized Louis's voice, and saw the same ragged scar on his hand as she'd seen on the robber when he signed the marriage license. She fled when she recognized him as one of the robbers. Unfortunately history doesn't tell us what happened next. In fact, Louis was a miner, but he supplemented his mining income by robbing stagecoaches with a couple of his friends.

And so, Hattie's story was born. A story of tragedy, love lost, hopes dashed and a little bit of the absurd.

I hope you enjoyed reading it! Stay tuned for more.

Warm regards,
Vivi Holt

About the Author

Vivi Holt was born in Australia. She grew up in the country, where she spent her youth riding horses at Pony Club, and adventuring through the fields and rivers around the farm. Her father was a builder, turned saddler, and her mother a nurse, who stayed home to raise their four children.

After graduating from a degree in International Relations, Vivi moved to Atlanta, Georgia to work for a year. It was there that she met her husband, and they were married three years later. She spent seven years living in Atlanta and travelled to various parts of the United States during that time, falling in love with the beauty of that immense country and the American people.

Vivi also studied for a Bachelor of Information Technology, and worked in the field until becoming a full-time writer in 2016. She now lives in Brisbane, Australia with her husband and three small children. Married to a Baptist pastor, she is very active in her local church.

Follow Vivi Holt
www.viviholt.com
vivi@viviholt.com

**WE HOPE YOU ENJOYED
THIS BOOK FROM**

LOVE INSPIRED

INSPIRATIONAL ROMANCE

Uplifting stories of faith, forgiveness and hope.

Fall in love with stories where faith helps
guide you through life's challenges, and discover
the promise of a new beginning.

6 NEW BOOKS AVAILABLE EVERY MONTH!

Addie kept monopolizing Evan's time. First at the B and B—though she could hardly blame herself for that. He was the one who'd insisted on helping her out. And now again at church. Surely he had better places to be than with her.

"Do you need to go?" she asked Evan. "Sorry I kept you so long."

"I'm not in a rush. I might pop out to Wilder Ranch for lunch with Jace and Mackenzie. After that I have to…" Evan groaned.

"Run into a burning building? Perform brain surgery? Teach a sewing class?"

Humor momentarily flashed across his features. "Go to a meeting for Old Westbend Weekend."

What? So much for some Evan-free time to pull herself back together. "I'm going to that, but I didn't realize you were. The B and B is one of the sponsors for the weekend." Addie had used her entire limited advertising budget for the three-day event.

"I thought my brother might block for me today. Instead he totally kicked me under the bus as it roared by. He caught Bill's attention and volunteered me for the hero thing." The pure torment on Evan's face was almost comical. "I want to back out of it, but Bill played the 'it's for the kids' card, and now I think I'm trapped."

"Look, Mommy!" Sawyer ran over to them. A grubby, slimy—and very dead—worm rested in the palm of his hand.

"Ew."

At her disgust, Sawyer showed the prize to Evan. "Good find. He looks like he's dead, though, so you'd better give him a proper burial."

"Yeah!" Sawyer hurried over to the patch of dirt. He plopped the worm onto the sidewalk and told it to "stay" just like he would Belay. That made both of them laugh. Then he used one of the sticks as a shovel and began digging a hole.

"He's like a cat, always bringing me dead animals as gifts. I'm surprised he doesn't leave them for me on the doorstep."

Evan chuckled while waving toward the parking lot. She turned to see his brother and Mackenzie walking to their vehicle.

"Do you guys want to come out to Wilder Ranch for lunch? I'm sure they wouldn't mind two more. It's a happy sort of chaos there with all of the kids."

Addie's heart constricted at the offer. No doubt Sawyer would love it. She wanted exactly what Evan was offering, but all of that was off-limits for her. She couldn't allow herself any more access into Evan's world or vice versa.

"We can't, but thanks. I've got to get Sawyer down for a nap." Addie wasn't about to attempt attending a meeting with a tired Sawyer, and she didn't have anywhere else in town for him to go.

Evan's face morphed from relaxed to taut, but he didn't press further. "Right. Okay. I guess I'll see you later then." After saying goodbye to Sawyer, he caught up with Jace and Mackenzie in the parking lot.

A momentary flash of loss ached in Addie's chest. A few days in Evan's presence and he was already showing her how different things could have been. It was like there was a life out there that she'd missed by taking the wrong path. It was shiny and warm and so, so out of reach.

And the worst of it was, until Evan, she hadn't realized just how much she was missing.

Don't miss
Her Hidden Hope *by Jill Lynn,*
available May 2020 wherever
Love Inspired books and ebooks are sold.

LoveInspired.com

LIEXP0420

*Officer Dante Santangelo doesn't "do" relationships,
but the busy single dad happily agrees to a secret
summer fling with younger free-spirited Gracie Bravo.
It's the perfect arrangement. Until Gracie realizes
she wants a life with Dante. Either she can say goodbye
at the end of the summer...or risk everything to
make this family happen.*

Read on for a sneak preview of
New York Times *bestselling author Christine Rimmer's
next book in the Bravos of Valentine Bay miniseries,*
Their Secret Summer Family.

"Gracie, will you look at me?"

Stifling a sigh, she turned her head to face him. Those
melty brown eyes were full of self-recrimination and
regret.

"I'm sorry," he said. "I never should have touched you.
I'm too old for you, and I'm not any kind of relationship
material, anyway. I don't know what got into me, but I
swear to you it's never going to happen again."

Hmm. How to respond?

Too bad there wasn't a large blunt object nearby. The
guy deserved a hard bop on the head. What was wrong
with him? No wonder it hadn't worked out with Marjorie.
The man didn't have a clue.

But never mind. Gracie held it together as he
apologized some more. She watched that beautiful mouth

move and pondered the mystery of how such a great guy could have his head so far up his own ass.

Maybe if she yanked him close and kissed him, he'd get over himself and admit that last night had been amazing, the two of them had off-the-charts chemistry and he didn't want to walk away from all that goodness, after all.

Yeah, kissing him might shut him up and get him back on track for more hot sexy times. It had worked more than once already.

But come on. She couldn't go jumping on him and smashing her mouth on his every time he started beating himself up for having a good time with her.

No. A girl had to have a little pride.

He thought last night was a mistake?

Fair enough. She'd actually let herself believe for a minute or two there that they had something good going on, that her long dry spell manwise might be over.

But never mind about that. Let him have it his way. She would agree with him.

And then she would show him exactly what he was missing. And then, when he couldn't take it anymore and begged her for another chance, she would say that they couldn't, that he was too old for her and it wouldn't be right.

Don't miss
Their Secret Summer Family *by Christine Rimmer,*
available May 2020 wherever
Harlequin Special Edition books and ebooks are sold.

Harlequin.com

HARLEQUIN

*Heartfelt or suspenseful,
inspiring or passionate, Harlequin
has your happily-ever-after.*

With new books published
every month, you are sure to find the
satisfying escape you know you deserve.

SIGN UP FOR THE HARLEQUIN NEWSLETTER

Be the first to hear about great new
reads and exciting offers!

Harlequin.com/newsletters